Autumn's Trail

Dorothy Bodoin

A Wings ePress, Inc.
Cozy Mystery Novel

Wings ePress, Inc.

Edited by: Jeanne Smith
Copy Edited by: Christie Kraemer
Executive Editor: Jeanne Smith
Cover Artist: Trisha FitzGerald-Jung

All rights reserved

Names, characters and incidents depicted in this book are products of the author's imagination or are used fictitiously. Any resemblance to actual events, locales, organizations, or persons, living or dead, is entirely coincidental and beyond the intent of the author or the publisher.

No part of this book may be reproduced or transmitted in any form or by any means, electronic or mechanical, including photocopying, recording, or by any information storage and retrieval system, without permission in writing from the publisher.

Wings ePress Books
www.wingsepress.com

Copyright © 2022 by: Dorothy Bodoin
ISBN-13:978-1-61309-966-7

Published In the United States Of America

Wings ePress Inc.
3000 N. Rock Road
Newton, KS 67114

Dedication

For Emilie Jeanne Bodoin, my dear niece and greatest fan.

* * *

One

A bold wave of yellow threaded its way through the green leaves that met across the curves of Spruce Road. Summer was winding down and school was looming, the long lazy days of making my own schedule almost over.

Like being able to attend this afternoon luncheon at Dark Gables, home of my friend, Foxglove Corners' renowned writer, Lucy Hazen.

Lucy and I had visited often during the summer, sharing reflections and tea leaf readings, but this afternoon promised to be different.

"There's a young woman I'd like you to meet, Jennet," Lucy had said. "Linnea Wilmott has a unique problem. I think you can help her solve it. It's a matter of time."

"That sounds intriguing. Can you tell me more?"

"I could, but you should hear it from Linnea. I've put together a light lunch for us," she'd added.

Wondering if I would have a new mystery to explore before school started, I turned into Lucy's driveway and slowed as I spied a deer leap out of the hedge of conifers on the right. It vanished into the woods in a blur of tan. Ahead stood Lucy's atmospheric country house, graceful gables rising up to a deep blue sky.

For a writer of horror stories slanted toward teenagers, Dark Gables was the perfect setting: remote and private. It had undoubtedly inspired many of Lucy's past works.

She stood on the porch to welcome me, her black hair arranged in an elegant chignon, her long black skirt billowing in a sudden breeze. Sunlight fell freely on her Zodiac charm bracelet and four gold chains.

I parked behind a white Tesla and climbed the stairs, pausing to pet Sky, Lucy's blue merle collie who wagged her tail happily in a greeting of her own.

With a jingle of her charms, Lucy said, "Welcome, Jennet. Our guest arrived just minutes ago. We're in the sunroom."

Bounding merrily down the dim hallway, Sky led us to a large, bright space at the end of the house where Lucy wrote her books and entertained infrequent visitors.

At our entrance, a young woman with long dark brown hair turned from the French doors through which she had been gazing at the fountain and the dark woods beyond the meadow. She was simply dressed in a blue knit shift with a flattering V neck and wore no jewelry except for an Apple watch and a gold medallion shaped like the head of a rough collie.

Ah! The collie connection. Doubtless Linnea's problem concerned a dog, possibly one who was lost.

I glanced at Lucy's luncheon with appreciation and surprise. She had moved a round table into the sunroom, covered it with a cheerful floral cloth, and set out a tempting repast of chicken salad, rolls, and lemonade. She'd used her best china and silver. This was truly an occasion, as we were usually quite casual, sitting on the wicker sofa and helping ourselves to tea and store-bought cookies.

Lucy made the introductions and shooed Sky away from the cream puffs which were perilously close to the table's edge.

"I'm so happy to meet you, Jennet," Linnea said. "I read all about you and your marvelous white collie in the paper last June."

She referred to Misty, one of my eight collies, whose discovery in Woodsboro Park had provided the solution to a decades-old mystery.

"Did you train her in search and rescue?" she asked.

"No," I said. "Misty is a natural. Like most dogs, she loves to dig holes."

She had other talents, but I didn't discuss them with anyone I didn't know well. I was growing increasingly curious about Lucy's purpose in bringing Linnea and me together.

Perhaps sensing my impatience, Lucy said, "Let's have lunch before the rolls cool off. Then we can talk. Everyone, have a seat."

I smiled as Sky took the command seriously, sitting as close to the dessert as she dared.

"It looks wonderful, Lucy," Linnea said, and indeed it was. Catered, I suspected, as Lucy considered cooking and fussing with food a drain on her writing time.

Having done justice to the luncheon, we moved to the patio and Lucy poured coffee, another departure. Tea was the official beverage of Dark Gables.

As she lifted her cup, the Zodiac charms sang in the silence. "Linnea is a fellow writer, Jennet," she said. "We met when she wrote me a fan letter."

Linnea nodded. "It was the first one I ever wrote, and it led to our friendship. Then in June, when I had a strange experience, I turned to Lucy."

"From time to time, strange things happen in Foxglove Corners," I said.

"Jennet calls Foxglove Corners the Home of the Strange and Ghostly," Lucy added. "She'll help you decide what you ought to do about it. If anything."

"I already know what I want to do," Linnea said. "I just don't know how to do it."

I'd seldom heard such an elaborate build-up to a tale, but then, Lucy was a mistress of suspense. Apparently, so was Linnea.

She took a sip of her coffee and began. "That day was so beautiful, I decided to go for a drive. I took Autumn and my camera and headed north on Huron Court. Then, in a heartbeat, everything changed."

I detected a subtle change in her tone, and with those words I knew what Linnea was going to say next. She seemed apprehensive. Even fearful. Huron Court was good at inspiring reactions like this.

"I had the air on and I was comfortable and relaxed," she said. "Suddenly a snowflake landed on the windshield. Then more. And still more. In the blink of an eye, I was driving through a snow squall."

She paused, frowning at my reaction or lack thereof. "You aren't surprised?"

"Not at all. That's what happened to me on Huron Court. That road has a light hold on the seasons."

And on time as well. But let Linnea tell her story in her own way.

"What do you mean?" she asked.

"Seasons change," I said. "From one second to the next. Without reason. Without warning."

"How did you find your way back to summer?" Lucy asked.

"I can't explain it, but the unnatural snow was only the beginning."

I sat back to listen to the rest of Linnea's story, assuming that her experience had been similar to mine.

I couldn't have been more wrong.

Two

"It kept snowing," Linnea said. "I was trapped in an absolute white-out. I couldn't see a foot in front of me."

"What did you do?" Lucy asked.

"I pulled to the side of the road and thought I'd wait it out, but it showed no signs of stopping. Finally, I turned around and headed back in the direction I'd come from. I hoped it wasn't snowing there, too. Whoever heard of snow in June?"

"It's rare," I said, adding silently, except on Huron Court.

"Eventually it tapered off. But I knew something was wrong when I saw Christmas decorations on a house I remembered passing. Only a short time ago I'd been admiring its vast flower garden.

"By then I was completely frazzled. Snow and Christmas decorations in mid-June? I saw a small diner with multi-colored lights around the door. I thought I'd have a hot drink and settle my nerves. I left Autumn in the car..."

She'd mentioned the name before. "Autumn?"

"My dog, my beautiful collie girl. I was only going to be gone a minute. I ordered coffee to go and glanced at the paper on the counter. I couldn't believe my eyes. The date was December 27, 1998.

I thought it must be a joke or one of those front-page reproductions of a momentous event like the end of World War Two. But the headlines seemed ordinary enough. I bought the paper," she added.

"Back in the car, I drank my coffee and started thinking. In 1998 I was still in college and living with my parents. If I had somehow traveled back in time, which seemed impossible, I wondered if I could live those years of my life over again. I had a sudden desire to see my old home and my mom and dad again. They've since passed on."

I took a sip of coffee and discovered it had turned into a cold drink. Still, I drank and reflected on my own time slip. The idea of visiting my family home had never occurred to me. When I had traveled in time, I'd never ventured out of Foxglove Corners.

Linnea went on. "On the way to Oakpoint, I noticed that everything looked different. There were just wooded acres where the Maplewood Mall is now, and Oakpoint was smaller with fewer houses and different businesses. The Oakpoint Classic Theater was showing *On the Beach*.

"All this time it was snowing, but lightly. When I reached my home, I parked across the street and just gazed at the house, hardly able to believe my eyes. It was exactly as I remembered, like an old photograph with the white picket fence around the front yard again and Dad's old Plymouth Volare parked in the driveway. I could see our Christmas tree through the window, but the lights were off. No one was home.

"Where had my family gone on December 27, 1998? It was so long ago I couldn't remember."

"How long did you stay in the past?" I asked.

"I'm not sure. That night, certainly, but I remember the sinking feeling of being out of place. I was virtually homeless. Another family would be living in the house I bought in 2000."

"But you obviously found your back to the present," Lucy said. "How did you do it?"

"I wish I knew. I only remember driving on Spruce Road, and it was summer again. I looked for the diner, thinking it might have acted as a conveyer of sorts, but it was gone."

She paused, appearing mesmerized by the play of light and water in Lucy's fountain.

"It happened to me," I said, "and also to two of my friends. We didn't go exploring in our past. We just wanted to go home. To our real home and year."

"I knew about Jennet's experiences," Lucy said, "but I never had one of my own, and thank heavens for that. I'm content to stay in my home, my time and life. As you may surmise, I stay well away from Huron Court."

Linnea said, "More than anything I want to go back. The world was fresher then. Even the coffee had more flavor.

"Just think how wonderful it would be to be able to live years of your life over. You could be with the loved ones you lost again. You could make different decisions, maybe even change your past..."

As she trailed off, lost in a blur of possibilities, I thought of my own life. I didn't regret any of my past decisions, but perhaps I was more fortunate than Linnea in her choices.

"If you made different decisions, your future would be different," I pointed out. "Maybe other things too. Are you familiar with Ray Bradbury's story, *A Sound of Thunder* and *the butterfly effect*?"

She nodded. "I'll be careful not to step on any butterflies. I only intend to change my own life. I have to go back."

"But you can't," I said. "Huron Court may have strange properties, but it isn't a time machine. You have no control over when it slips off its axis, or if it does, or where it sends you."

"Think, Linnea," Lucy added. "You might wind up forty years in the future. What then? Or what if you eliminated yourself?"

Linnea set her cup down on the table with excessive force. "But I don't have a choice. I left Autumn there, back in 1998."

Apparently we'd reached the heart of the matter, the problem. A lost dog. Autumn had been noticeably absent from Linnea's narrative. I was a member of the Lakeville Collie Rescue League, a finder of dogs in distress. In that role, Lucy had thought I could help Linnea. Or so I assumed.

"How did that happen?" I asked.

"Again, I'm not sure. After I saw my old house in Oakpoint, my memories are fuzzy. I remember driving away in the snow. It was getting late. I needed to find a motel that would take dogs.

"At one point I swerved on ice and hit something. I don't know what, and never found out. I got out of the car to investigate and left the door open. Then I heard a crash like thunder. That's when Autumn dashed out of the car. I called her, but the storm must have spooked her. She ran off into the night and the snow and disappeared."

"If your memories are fuzzy, how do you know whether this happened in the past or present?" I asked.

"I'm pretty sure it was in the past. In 1998."

She didn't say what convinced her. Pretty sure wasn't positive, and whether in the past or present, Autumn was still missing.

I was almost afraid to ask, but I did. "How can I help you, Linnea?"

"Show me how to get back to 1998," she said.

Three

It was as if Linnea hadn't heard our cautions, or more likely heard them and cast them aside.

"I can't do that," I said. "There's no handy 'How To' guide. Even if we had one, I wouldn't risk getting swept away in the time winds."

Linnea sighed. "I've been trying all summer to find the way back. Every day I drive up and down Huron Court, all the way to the cemetery and back. I've even taken that parallel road. Nothing ever happens."

"Because it isn't meant to be," Lucy said.

I wondered if Lucy had ever read Linnea's tea leaves. We were drinking coffee, but the teapot and tins of tea were always close at hand.

Lucy said, "All sorts of calamities might arise if you returned to the past. You were lucky before."

"Except, remember, I lost Autumn."

"There is that, but I don't think the presence of a single dog out of time could have any dire effect on the future," Lucy added.

Linnea said, "If you can't help me, Jennet, I guess I'll have to keep on haunting Huron Court and hope for the best."

I cringed at her use of the word 'haunt,' imagining her on Huron Court—where I would never be. She would stop at the wildflower meadow, planted on the site of a Victorian house that had burned to the ground, unable to resists its colors and fragrances. She would ask me to help her get home to the future.

Playing in time was too dangerous, as we had tried to explain to her. Dangerous for her and others as well.

Linnea stole a glance at her watch, that large futuristic accessory. "This has been lovely, Lucy, but I have to leave. I just remembered something I had to do."

I doubted that, but what did it matter? Linnea had made her strange request, we had attempted to deflate it, and the episode was over. I hoped so.

"But before I go, I have something I want to leave with you." She pulled a slender blue book out of her purse and handed it to me. The picture of a beautiful sable and white collie graced the cover. "It's a journal, a record of all my experiences, starting with the first time I was aware that something was wrong. Maybe if you read it, you'll change your mind about helping me."

"Thank you," I said. "But please don't count on it. Don't count on me."

Lucy saw Linnea out and returned to the sunroom. "I thought Linnea only wanted to share her experience with us, to be convinced that she wasn't going out of her mind. I never dreamed she wanted to go back to the past."

"If she continues to drive on Huron Court, she may succeed," I said. "I think this is about more than finding Autumn. Well..." I gathered the empty cups and set them on the coffee service tray. "It's been interesting. I feel bad about Autumn. One way or the other, she's gone."

A dog abandoned in time, searching desperately for her owner. In my years with collie rescue, I had never dealt with a problem like this. I had to remind myself that in real time Autumn would be long dead.

~ * ~

I live on Jonquil Lane with my husband, Deputy Sheriff Crane Ferguson, and our eight collies, all but one of whom I'd rescued. We have a green Victorian farmhouse with a stained-glass window between gables and ten acres of land, a portion of which is planted with colorful annuals and perennials.

In my view, ours is the most beautiful house in Foxglove Corners.

My reception committee waited impatiently in the living room, eight gorgeous collies vying for space at the front window. Their faces disappeared as I parked, and I knew they'd be racing to be the first to welcome me, to receive the first caress.

I opened the side door and in an instant was enveloped in a swirl of collie colors: blue, white, shades of sable, and black. I dispensed biscuits, poured fresh water, and took the pack outside to play. While they found their favorite toys and engaged in mock battles, I gazed at them fondly. My family.

Once, when she was my only dog, I had lost Halley. I remembered how grim those days had been, how drained of color and joy. Ultimately we had been reunited, but what if our separation had been permanent? Suppose I'd never known what had happened to her?

If one of my dogs were lost, I'd do everything in my power to find her. Even if she were lost in time. I was, after all, a dedicated member of Collie Rescue.

I resolved to give Linnea the help she'd requested. Exactly how I was going to find the missing Autumn eluded me for the moment.

~ * ~

By the time Crane came home, I had a beef stew simmering on the stove and the ingredients for a salad spread out on the kitchen counter.

The dogs were in welcome mode again, circling around him with flattened ears and wagging tails. Candy was nudging his knee and yelping as if to air her day's grievances.

He waded through the onslaught and kissed me, wrapping me in the enticing scents of the outdoors.

Crane has gray eyes flecked with frost needles and silvery strands in his blond hair. In his uniform with its gleaming badge, he looks as if he is lost in time himself, having stepped out of the Old West into my country kitchen. That was my fantasy, my happy version of the American dream.

Mindful of the dangers that went along with his profession, I always breathed more easily when he was safe at home.

"Did anything interesting happen today?" I asked.

"Not especially. It was long and hot. I'm glad to be home."

As I was glad to have an intriguing tale to tell.

"I had lunch with Lucy and met a young woman with a very unusual problem," I said.

I told him about Linnea Wilmot, the latest person to fall under the spell of Huron Court. At least I assumed she was the latest. The wayfarers who slipped into another time while traveling on that accursed road don't usually broadcast their experiences for fear they'll be dismissed as delusional.

"She wants to go back to 1998. She left her collie, Autumn, there, and she wants me to help her."

He smiled, no doubt remembering my aversion to Huron Court coupled with my dedication to collie rescue.

"What did you tell her?"

"That, unfortunately, I couldn't help her."

"But you're going to."

He knew me too well.

"I didn't tell her yet, but I'm going to try. It'll be a last hurrah before school starts."

He was still smiling. "Because of the collie?"

"Mostly."

Four

The next morning, I set out for Clovers where I knew Annica, my young partner-in-detection, would be working. She counted on her waitressing job and scholarships to cover the cost of college tuition and books.

Brent's and Annica's engagement party at the Hunt Club Inn was this weekend. I wanted to talk about dresses with Annica and also tell her about Linnea and her time travel project.

The leaves were turning from green to gold in the woods on Crispian Road, but the clovers that bordered the little restaurant were as bright as emeralds and looked freshly painted. Here, at least, we could hold on to summer.

Annica was on a break, sitting alone at a booth with a cup of coffee at her elbow, her attention fixed on the woods across the road. These days she was as radiant as the ruby and diamond engagement ring she'd received from Foxglove Corner's renowned fox hunting bachelor, Brent Fowler. Her pink dress complemented her red-gold hair and the tiny earrings made to match her custom-made ring.

She snapped out of her daydream as soon as I joined her.

"Just look at the trees," she said. "Pretty soon you won't be able to drop in at all times of the day."

Classes to control and teach, a long commute, evenings given over to lesson plans. Vacation time was almost over. "Don't remind me."

Marcy, her fellow waitress, appeared to take my order. I'd planned on having a cup of hot chocolate, but the blueberry pancake special looked too good to pass up.

"I'll be busy, too," Annica said. "New courses and planning our wedding."

"Are you at the planning stage already?"

"It's going to be small, but there's still lots to do. First I'm going to find the perfect wedding gown."

"Then I guess you won't have time to help me with my new mystery."

Her eyes lit up as they always did at the prospect of an adventure. "I'll find the time. Tell me about it."

"It deals with another lost dog—with a difference."

Earlier this summer, we had rescued a dog stolen from Woodsboro Park during a crowded event. That had been difficult enough, but Autumn presented a more formidable challenge.

"But that's impossible for so many reasons," Annica said when I explained Linnea's goal. "It's not like you can go through a door to a specific year."

"No, but I've been thinking."

In truth, I'd thought of little else. "Linnea was vague about returning to the present. She slipped back to a December day in 1998 and all she remembers is driving through snow. She claims she inadvertently left Autumn behind in the past at a time when a snow squall was turning into a thunderstorm. But what if it happened after she returned to the present? Then we'd have a simple case of a dog lost in the Huron Court area."

"That's a load of assumptions," Annica said. "By the way, what does Autumn look like?"

I frowned, realizing that I didn't know. Linnea hadn't described Autumn or shown me a picture of her.

"Let's see. Judging from her name, she's a sable."

And there I had to stop as a barrage of reasonable questions clamored in my mind. Golden or dark mahogany? A full white collar or colored fur breaking through her ruff? Distinctive markings or characteristics like a blue eye? Tipped or pricked ears? How old was she, for heaven's sake?

"I have to talk to Linnea again," I said.

"As of now, we have nothing to go on," Annica pointed out. "What are the chances of time traveling at all, let alone to a specific year? I'd say zero."

I couldn't resist teasing her. "Did you change your mind about helping me?"

"Not a chance."

"That's the spirit," I said.

Anyone could solve an ordinary mystery. The ones that came my way were often wrapped in a cloak of impossibility. If finding Autumn was to be my last hurrah, let it be a memorable one.

"I bought a new dress for the party," I said, happy to be on firmer ground. "It's clover green with an empire style waist and lace trim."

"Mine is red." Annica twirled her ring gently. "I still can't believe Brent and I are engaged. I'm afraid I'll wake up one morning and find it's only a dream."

I remembered feeling the same way. "It's a dream come true."

~ * ~

I still had no idea how to help Linnea travel back to the past, and I worried constantly about what she intended to do in 1998, which of her decisions would be different, and how a different choice would affect her and possibly others as well.

The butterfly effect again. Dinosaurs roaming through Foxglove Corners.

I didn't worry too much about my lack of a plan. Who said we'd be able to travel to the past?

Crane had an idea that surprised me as he didn't often interfere in my mysterious endeavors.

"We can scope out Huron Court," he said. "See if it's still a springboard to different times."

'We,' he'd said. I had no intention of setting foot—or car—on the accursed road alone. But if we were together…

We'd gone before and stayed firmly anchored in the present time.

"I haven't seen the wildflower meadow all summer," I said. "I'd like to."

I'd never even thought about it. After the pink Victorian burned to the ground, Brent had bought the land and scattered plants and seeds at random on the site. What happened next was truly amazing.

The flowers had flourished, growing thick and lush, obliterating the patio stone paths Brent had set out in the rows between them. Every year they reseeded themselves and grew larger and more vibrant. Strangely, some of them defied identification.

Think Jack-in-the-beanstalk.

"But what will that accomplish?" I asked.

"You'll be able to tell Linnea that the time switch appears to be disabled."

Which she would believe, after having driven up and down Huron Court countless times. Would she then abandon her attempts to return to the past?

"All right," I said. "As long as you go with me."

I always felt safe with him.

"We'll go on Sunday," he said.

Five

On Saturday evening, we attended Brent's and Annica's engagement party at the Hunt Club Inn.

Red was the predominant color of the evening. Candles and roses and a four-tiered cake decorated with a make-believe russet colored fox asleep in a bed of berries. He consisted of sugar and food coloring and had the grace to look man-made unlike the Inn's stuffed fox head. Brent had reserved a large private room well away from that monstrosity.

We were a gathering of friends: Lucy Hazen; Leonora, my fellow English teacher at Marston High School and her husband, Jake; Camille and her husband, Crane's Uncle Gilbert; and the men who worked at Brent's barn. All of the people who had been a part of my life.

We had dined on prime beef, lake trout for those who didn't care for meat, and Crane was beginning his second piece of cake. The toasts were over, the mood was festive, and Annica was considerably calmer. She'd confided to me about being uneasy as the center of attention.

How unlike her, but then she'd never been engaged before.

She came up to me silently, a half-smile on her face.

"Jennet, would you go to the restroom with me, please?" she asked. "My hair is misbehaving in back."

I glanced at her, seeing no signs of disorder in her red-gold curls and swirls. "It looks fine to me."

"I need some help."

I rose. "Excuse me, Crane. I'll be right back."

As we walked away, she drew me behind a pillar and lowered her voice. "She's here tonight. That Alethea Venn woman."

Alethea, Brent's long-time fox-hunting friend, who happened to be beautiful and arrogant and rude, looked on Brent as her property, even though I didn't think they saw each other apart from hunting and related activities. Even though she was older than Brent.

"Surely Brent didn't invite her," I said.

"She's not one of our party. Anyone can dine at the Hunt Club Inn. What'll I do?"

"You don't have to do anything. If she sees you, say hello. She'll soon realize you're engaged. Accept her congratulations."

"I don't want to see her," she said.

"Maybe you won't."

"She's like the wicked fairy who comes to the feast to cast a spell on the fair maiden."

I hid a smile. Annica was serious. That magnificent ring and Brent's proposal should give her all the confidence she needed.

I said, "Your hair is perfect, isn't it?"

"I guess. The last time I saw Alethea, she was so rude to me. She just talked to Brent like I was invisible."

Althea was an expert at snubbing people she considered inferior, among them animal activists. I'd been on the receiving end of her vitriol several times.

"Let's go back to the table and hope for the best," I said. "But Annica, she's bound to find out about your engagement. Didn't your mom send an announcement in to the *Banner*?"

"They didn't print it yet."

"Well, take heart. She can't do anything to change it."

"She's bad luck. She'll ill-wish us."

I was tempted to smile again, to laugh at Annica's melodramatic fairy tale rhetoric, but I didn't. She was seriously upset.

"We have Lucy to counteract any spell she might cast," I said.

But my sympathies were with Annica. Alethea could be unpleasant. Knowing her as well as I cared to, I thought that was a given. Wicked fairy, indeed.

I hoped she wouldn't discover we were at the Inn, only in a different room.

~ * ~

She found us, of course, strode into the room Brent had reserved as if she owned the Inn. She stared at what was left of the cake, a sliver saved from the top that proclaimed: Congratulations Annica and Brent.

She stood there like the wicked fairy of Annica's imagining, more like a witch in black, with her hair streaming down her back, longer and redder than I'd ever seen it. Her elaborate choker looked as if it contained a genuine emerald and diamonds. I was sure it did.

"This is a surprise," she said. "Why didn't I know about it?"

How could Brent answer that question?

"You were in North Carolina all summer," he said. "You know now."

It was as good an answer as any.

He reached for Annica's hand. "It's always been Annica for me."

I held my breath.

Obviously, Alethea didn't agree. She wasn't going to answer. Conversation at the table went from muted to non-existent. People focused on their dessert. Lucy frowned.

Cast your spell, I thought.

Her eyes fixed on Brent, Alethea said, "Congratulations."

She might as well have said, "Curse you."

With that one ice-encased word, she retreated, leaving a collective breath of relief in her wake.

Annica came to life, her face suffused with color. "She did it again. She ignored me."

"Forget Althea," Brent said. "That's just her way."

"I hope we've seen the last of her."

"We'll leave her off the wedding list." Brent's voice was louder than normal, intentionally, I felt, but Alethea couldn't possibly have heard him.

Annica said, "There's a duplicate cake in the kitchen. We want everyone to take a piece home."

And so she returned us to party mode.

But afterward, as we lingered together at the deserted table, Annica said, "I have an enemy. She's going to disrupt our wedding."

Here was my first task as matron-of-honor, to assure the bride-to-be that all would be well.

"She doesn't like to lose. No one does, but she can't do anything about it."

"Short of murder."

"That's too tame for Alethea. If you run into her in the future, expect her to ignore you. You don't have to worry about Brent. He made it clear where he stands, and it's with you."

"Yes, that's true," she murmured.

"It'll be all right," I promised, but privately hoped Alethea would accept defeat with a modicum of grace. Really, what else could she do?

Six

As soon as we turned on Huron Court the next morning, I noticed the haze and the sudden cessation of sound. It's always quiet in the country, but we should be hearing something. Birdsong, rustlings, a disturbance in the air, however slight.

Do normal sounds disappear when something unearthly is present?

I closed my eyes and opened them again. The haze was still there. Huron Court was known for its mists, not haze. Well, we had haze today.

"Maybe this was a bad idea," I said.

"Why?"

"Something's off. Can't you sense it?"

"I don't. What exactly?"

I looked out the window, hoping to see a fleeting sign of wildlife. A bird or perhaps a sly fox. Nothing moved. It was as if we had driven off the face of the earth into a painted backdrop. Plants frozen in motionless air, still shadows, a subtle blurring. The world appeared to hold its breath. Waiting.

"I can't explain it," I said. "Call it a feeling."

"It's just Huron Court being Huron Court. This is a lonely, godforsaken stretch."

"Maybe. Let's turn around while we still can."

I was suddenly afraid, even though Crane was sitting next to me, within grabbing distance.

It's too late.

"All right, if that's what you want to do," Crane said. "But I think we're okay."

Before he could turn the SUV around, the hum of a motor slid into the silence. The vehicle was close behind us.

Well, you were looking for sound.

"We have company," he said, steering to the roadside. "Let's wait and see who it is."

The hum grew louder, still separated from us by the last long curve. Most likely another traveler was taking advantage of a picture-perfect summer day, a driver unaware of Huron Court's dicey reputation.

No car appeared, and abruptly the hum vanished, cut off as sharply as a recording stilled by a power failure.

Crane scanned the section of road we'd just passed. "What happened?"

"The car stopped?"

That was the best explanation, the most logical one. But when was Huron Court logical? Furthermore, why would anyone stop on the side of a country road?

To take pictures, perhaps? That made sense. We could turn around and investigate, but to what end? Would there be anything to see?

I had an uneasy suspicion that whoever had shared the road with us had been gobbled up by rapacious Time. If so, Time had its victim for the day. Its quota. We were safe.

"What the devil happened to that car?" Crane asked.

"I can't imagine. It's best to leave the hum in the realm of the weird."

We had planned to make a stop at the wildflower meadow, and it was minutes away. Another curve, and a kaleidoscope of fantastic mixed colors broke through the unrelenting green.

Crane parked the SUV and I walked up to the meadow's edge, mesmerized by the floral show. He slipped his arm around my waist. The haze was heavy over the flowers, and my apprehension had faded.

"It's so beautiful," I said.

Exotic flowers covered every inch of the meadow. Blossoms as blue as bachelor's buttons that resembled vining roses with no trellis to climb; orange-red lilies taller than any lily I'd ever seen, even those in Camille's garden, and daisy-like plants that looked like purple coneflowers except for their height. From where I stood, they looked taller than Crane.

Crane said, "Brent must have scattered seeds from a magic package."

"He never gave the plants any food or fertilizer. He just let them grow, and grow they did."

Up to the sky?

Not quite; not yet.

All these enchanting blooms, and I didn't have the slightest desire to gather a bouquet. Every single flower belonged exclusively to this meadow. Remove one, and it would die.

Still, I was glad we'd come this way today. Except…

Why had I wanted to revisit Huron Court, aside from seeing if anything would happen?

That was my only reason, and all I'd learned was that haze had replaced the road's signature mist, it was unnaturally quiet, and we'd stayed in our own time.

Don't forget the car, the day's unsolved mystery.

While I took several pictures of the flowers with my phone, Crane said, "Did Linnea mention what part of Huron Court she was on when she drove into the past?"

I couldn't remember if she'd seen the wildflower meadow. "I don't think so. She talked about a house with Christmas decorations, but that was after, when it was winter."

"There are no houses on Huron Court," Crane pointed out.

"Not anymore, and it has only one landmark, this meadow."

"I guess it doesn't matter," Crane said. "Do you believe her?"

"I do. We know it's possible to slide into another time, and it's unlikely anyone would concoct such a wild story if it hadn't really happened."

I couldn't recall any tales about Huron Court. No one had notified the papers of an out-of-time experience or spread rumors, whereas people spoke freely about ghostly apparitions in Foxglove Corners.

I took one more picture and frowned. Something didn't look right. What?

"Does the meadow seem larger to you?" I asked.

"A little. Over time, flowers reseed themselves and spread out."

He was right. I had ample evidence of that in the garden I tended. Not everything has a supernatural explanation.

"You'll have to convince Linnea that you can't help her," Crane said. "If she wants to change her past, she'll have to do it alone."

"But the dog... Autumn."

"There's no dog here today."

Unless she roamed the Huron Court acres howling her misery under another summer's sun.

I slipped my phone back in my pocket. If only I wasn't afraid to raid the meadow. Those blue rose-like flowers would look so pretty on the kitchen table.

I looked back at them and the flowers had vanished. In their place stood the pink Victorian, Violet's house that had burned.

It can't be

I looked again.

It wasn't.

The flowers, all of them, the riot of color, were back. The transformation had lasted no longer than a heartbeat.

"Are you all right, honey?" Crane asked. "You look like you just saw a ghost."

"I thought I saw Violet's house for a minute," I said.

"It's the haze," he added with a wink.

"I'd better make an appointment to have my eyes checked before school starts."

"Yes, and we'd better be on our way."

Seven

On the way home, I looked for the car whose hum had been so summarily cut off. There was no other vehicle on Huron Court, which made me think it might have driven into the past or the future. Because there had been a car behind us. Both of us had heard it.

What was one more inexplicable happening on this road of mystery?

Later that day, after dinner, I opened Linnea's journal with all the anticipation I felt when beginning a new Gothic novel. This one had the advantage of being true. Linnea and I were having lunch together this week, and I wanted to know every detail of her time trip before then, even though I wasn't going to help her return to the past.

Would there be anything new in her journal, details she hadn't already told us? Well, I'd soon know. Taking a sip of cocoa, I began reading:

LINNEA'S JOURNAL

This is an account of what happened to me on a hot, sunny day in June while I was enjoying a drive in the country. It started to snow! At first I thought a piece of dandelion fluff landed on my windshield, but it was a snowflake, and there were more. In minutes all I could see was white. The woods and the road in front of me, everything, had gone instantly from summer to winter.

When the temperature hovered in the low eighties? It wasn't possible. But it was happening. I turned on the windshield wipers and realized I was in the middle of a snowstorm.

I remembered wondering if a flying saucer had crashed on earth and this disruption in the weather was the fallout. It might not be so dramatic, but something was very wrong.

The road was slippery. When I skidded into the brush that grew at the roadside and realize how close I'd come to a significant drop, I sat in the car for a few minutes, letting it idle, while I tried to stop shaking. I turned on the radio. There was nothing but static.

What could I do?

When I'd turned on this road, which I later learned was Huron Court, the sun was shining and the sky was clear. Wildflowers were blooming. In other words, it was a typical June day.

I asked myself why couldn't I turn around and drive back into summer? So that's what I did. It didn't work.

This ungodly winter storm was everywhere. The old white house on the hilltop which I'd passed half an hour ago, admiring its large flower garden, was surrounded by snow. What was even odder were the multi-colored lights on the evergreens in front and outlining the door. Christmas decorations in an impossible winter. What next?

I felt like I'd landed in the Twilight Zone or that I was dreaming, because in real life seasons don't change in the blink of an eye.

Actually, I didn't know what to think, except that if I'd never turned on that road, this wouldn't be happening. Whether I could understand what was going on or not, I had to deal with it.

So I kept driving, entered the freeway, and headed to Oakpoint. I would go home and hope I'd find everything the way I'd left it, with green grass and flowers and sunshine. The radio would start working, and there'd be a simple explanation for the strangest phenomenon anyone ever experienced.

~ * ~

I looked up from the page to find my mug on the floor, lying on its side, drained of cocoa. Misty's whiskers had a suspicious chocolate sheen. I'd forgotten a cardinal rule of collie ownership: don't leave anything sweet unattended. Dogs and chocolate don't mix, but Misty was a big dog. She should be all right.

I turned my attention to a feeling that had crept up on me as I'd read Linnea's account. Something was wrong; something was off. It was similar to the feeling I'd had in the wildflower meadow.

"Is your book good?" Crane asked, refolding the *Banner*.

"It's Linnea's journal, and yes, it's interesting. She writes clearly, but..."

Suddenly the 'off' element crystalized.

"Linnea said she went for a ride with her dog, Autumn, but she doesn't mention her, not once. If I were driving with one of our collies, there would be plenty to talk about. Candy would try to take over the passenger's seat. Star might get sick. Velvet would keep barking, wanting attention. Linnea's story reads like she's alone in the car."

"Maybe she doesn't consider Autumn part of the story," he said.

"But one of the reasons she gave for wanting to return to the past was Autumn. She claims she left her there."

"I'll ask you again. Do you think this lady is telling the truth about her time trip?"

"I did. I can't see any reason for her to lie about it. And how would she know about time travel and Huron Court?"

"It's unlikely she would."

"This doesn't have to be a mystery," I said. "I'll ask Linnea about Autumn when we meet for lunch."

"And I'll take the dogs out," Crane said.

I picked up my empty mug, held it in front of Misty's face, and told her half-heartedly that she was a naughty dog. She raised her head, gave me her most endearing innocent look, and joined the other dogs who had gathered from far and wide to prance at Crane's side, waiting for their last walk of the day to materialize.

I could have continued reading, but I wanted to finish the rest of the journal in one evening and had run out of time. Before proceeding, I wanted to think about Autumn.

If this were my journal, I couldn't record the events of a single evening without mentioning one of our own collies.

Where was Autumn while Linnea was slip-sliding her way through an unnatural winter?

Eight

The next day hot, humid weather settled over Foxglove Corners. It sapped my energy and turned eight exuberant collies into limp plush replicas of themselves. Early, before the temperature climbed even higher, I took a pitcher of lemonade and a glass out to the porch planning to read more of the journal. The dogs joined me but took care to lie in the shade.

LINNEA'S JOURNAL

To my great disappointment, it was winter in Oakpoint. Christmas ornamentation transformed houses into glittering holiday fantasies. Icicle lights dripped down on reindeer families and Santas, and I viewed all decorations, both tacky and tasteful, through a veil of falling snow.

The radio was suddenly working, playing Christmas songs and carols. When I finally found a voice, it delivered disturbing news: a weather alert. The snow was continuing through the day and into the evening. We could expect an additional four inches. Not a word about the bizarre summer snowfall.

As much as I wanted to go home, I also dreaded what I might find there.

So when I saw a small restaurant, Jill's Country Oven, I pulled in the lot. I planned to unwind over a hot drink and not dwell on the fact that I'd driven down this street countless times and never noticed a restaurant there.

Not until I got out of the car did I realize I was dressed for summer in jeans and a sleeveless tank top. The cold burned my arms and face, and the snow flew in my eyes, blinding me. I didn't have anything to protect myself, not an emergency rain jacket or sweater or even a blanket. Fortunately, there were only about a dozen steps to the restaurant. I wouldn't have time to freeze.

A real Christmas tree decorated with red ornaments and silver tinsel stood in the entrance. The few people who sat at tables followed me with their eyes, uttering comments I couldn't hear. I went straight to the counter where a young waitress with brown braids wound on top of her head stared at me.

"You poor girl," she said. "Did you get robbed or something?"

"Something like that," I said.

"Did you call the police?"

"I'm on my way to the station now. I just came in for a cup of coffee."

"Coming right up," she said. "You can't go back out there dressed like that. I think I can find something for you in the lost-and-found."

She poured my coffee and disappeared in a back room, returning with a parka. It was an ugly mustard color and had an unsightly stain running from the collar to the pocket. She held it up. "Nobody's coming back for this. What do you think?"

"It's better than nothing. Thanks." I noticed the parka had a hood. I could wear it over my shoulders like a cape until I got home where my own winter clothes were packed away for the season.

"This snow is a surprise," I ventured.

"Not really. They've been talking about it all week. Looks like a white New Year's Eve."

I had been looking forward to a Fourth of July barbecue.

The waitress turned to another customer. When I finished my coffee, I glanced at the bill. I brought a dollar out of my wallet, left it on the counter, and stood. Ignoring laughter that I suspected was directed toward me, I settled the pathetic borrowed coat over my shoulder.

On the way to the exit, I noticed a stack of newspapers next to a sign cut into a Christmas tree shape that said 'Free.' As I helped myself to one, my hand froze on the date: December 27, 1998.

That couldn't be. The snow had done something to my eyes, made them water. But the letters and numbers didn't change. The year was 1998—unless this was a sick joke.

It had to be a nightmare. Here I was dressed for a summer outing with a ratty borrowed coat over my shoulders in a restaurant that didn't exist. I was about to go out into a snowstorm that couldn't be.

All I'd need would be to find that my car had disappeared like it did in a recurring dream of mine.

But no. The car was where I'd parked it, covered with a good inch of snow, and the scraper was in the garage at home.

I cleared the windows with my hands, then sat inside with the heater on, skimming the paper as if it held a clue to the impossible situation I found myself in.

The articles were unremarkable. A plane crash in the Upper Peninsula. An ice fisherman missing for the second day. The Oakpoint Playhouse's auditions for their production of *The Admirable Chrichton*. Nothing helpful, but I kept turning pages. Anything to delay going home. I was afraid. I expected the worst.

~ * ~

I drank my lemonade and basked in the growing heat of the day, imagining myself trapped in sub-zero weather without a coat or head covering. Poor Linnea. But I'd read thirty pages of her journal and, again, hadn't come across a single reference to Autumn.

I assume Linnea had left her dog in the car during her stop at Jill's Country Oven. Wasn't Autumn thirsty, too, and hungry? Why would Linnea omit details that any normal person would include?

What happened when she finally arrived home? I couldn't remember what she had told Lucy and me. As I turned the page, the dogs transformed themselves into a wild, yipping, howling pack. Their tails were wagging, and the white car that turned in our driveway had long green fins.

I was momentarily disconcerted, thinking how strange it would be if we had all slipped back to 1998, until I remembered that cars with fins were long gone by then.

Brent Fowler had found a Plymouth Belvedere in good condition and lovingly restored it. If you turned on the tape deck, you would hear his favorite songs from the sixties.

Brent would have loved to have an experience like Linnea's.

He took a shopping bag illustrated with puppies and bones from the back seat and made his way through the collie welcoming committee, dispensing pats but keeping the treats out of the reach of long noses.

"Morning, Jennet," he said. "What are you reading?"

"The journal Linnea wrote about her time trip," I said.

He set the shopping bag on the wicker table and dropped into the chair next to mine. I told him about my major concern.

"She doesn't even mention Autumn who was right there with her all the time."

"That's the dog we're going to help her find?"

I nodded. "The dog she claims she left in the past. I'm beginning to wonder."

"I think she's nuts," Brent said.

"Based on what?"

"Most people would be traumatized if they were taken out of their time and dumped in the past. They wouldn't be trying to go back."

"I suppose it depends on the person," I said. "How inquisitive she is, how brave, how enterprising..."

"How nutty. There's no way we're going to be able to go back in time to look for a lost dog."

"We've done the impossible before," I said.

But I agreed with him. "Autumn may be lost in our own time."

"Then we're just looking for a lost dog. We can do that."

"Let's go inside," I said. "I have another pitcher of lemonade and other cold drinks."

I opened the door, and the dogs trooped in with us. In the kitchen I gave them fresh water and Brent a ginger ale.

"If you could go back in time and change something in your life, one of your decisions, for example, would you do it?" I asked.

He didn't have to think about it. "I don't have any regrets. Everything I ever did brought me to where I am today, and I'm exactly where I want to be, with Annica. What about you?"

"I feel the same way. Obviously Linnea doesn't. I wish I knew what she wanted to change."

"She can want all she likes," Brent said. "It's not going to happen."

I wasn't so sure.

Nine

After Brent left, I picked up the journal and found myself back in Linnea's world, battling snowy streets and a nightmare come true.

LINNEA'S JOURNAL-continued
While the newspaper definitely reflected the world of December, 1998, I wasn't convinced that I had somehow time-traveled to that year. Not without a machine or device or cataclysmic event like a rogue lightning strike.

Could someone be playing an elaborate trick on me?

However comforting compared to the alternative, that seemed unlikely. Who could know I'd stop at a restaurant and happen to see a fake newspaper? And where had that restaurant come from? Jill's Country Oven. I'd swear I'd never seen it before, neither in the present nor the past. Was it part of the hoax?

No one would be that invested in pranking me. I would swear to that, too.

I had delayed the inevitable long enough. The car was warm, the windshield wipers had done their job, and nothing stopped me from going forward to meet head-on whatever came next. I set the newspaper on the seat beside me and drove out to the road, which wasn't yet plowed or salted.

I saw several signs that this was not the season's first snowfall. In fact, a large snowman with a long carrot nose presided over a spacious front yard on Main Street.

As I drove along, I watched for unfamiliar sights like houses or stores I didn't remember. With regard to the houses, it was hard to tell through the falling snow and holiday decorations. Who looks at every single house in the neighborhood? Who would remember any changes over the years, especially when viewed through falling snow?

I was surprised I hadn't thought of this before, but if the year was 1998, my house hadn't been built yet. There were no warm winter clothes packed away. None of my possession were waiting for me. Most of them hadn't been acquired yet. If it was 1998, I was living with my parents and going to college.

So that was my destination, my parents' bungalow on Wallace Street.

I'll admit I was so frazzled by the shock of being toppled from my normal place in the universe that everything looked the same to me and, at the same time, everything looked different. With one telling exception.

New owners had recently painted the Dutch colonial in the middle of Wallace Street beige with dark brown trim, but for years it had been a garish shade of bright blue. As I passed it, I saw that it was blue again.

And so I arrived at my parents' house. The interior was dark, the driveway empty. Being afraid of fire, my mother never left a light on when she was away from home. I could see the outline of a heavily decorated Christmas tree—our tree—in the bay window.

I parked across the street and sat in the idling car, thinking. Wondering. Where had my parents gone on December 27, 1998?

To visit Grandma?

Why wasn't I with them? Where was I?

Would I find myself inside asleep in my bedroom?

At seven-thirty?

Of course not. My car, a silver Taurus, was nowhere in sight.

Wasn't there a time-travel rule about not coming face to face with yourself—in this case, with your younger self—when visiting the past lest you zap yourself out of existence? Or was that only in science-fiction stories?

If only I could have knocked on the door and seen my mother. I'd tell her what happened. She would believe me, I knew. Mothers make everything all right.

But I couldn't do that. I pictured myself appearing at the door in jeans and a parka in a color I never wore. My hair was a few inches longer these days, and I was using less make-up. At least that was so when I had set out this morning.

"I'm your daughter," I would say. "I've come from the future. I don't know how it happened. I don't belong here. Please help me go back to my rightful time."

Would any mother believe that?

It didn't matter. No one was home, and I couldn't sit in the car indefinitely waiting for my family. And what if some nosy neighbor reported me to the police? And what if—this was the first time it had occurred to me—someone noticed that my car was a futuristic model and my driver's license bore the wrong date?

I finally decided I couldn't interact with my parents yet. I had to think. What could I do? What did I want to do?

The answer was simple. With all my heart I wanted to return to my own time, to cruise the countryside without a care, to never have driven into that godforsaken snowstorm.

Was that possible?

Wishes wouldn't see me safely through the night, though. I had to find a place to stay, a motel that allowed dogs and didn't ask awkward questions.

Autumn had no idea of the trouble we were in. As long as we were together, everything would be all right.

~ * ~

At last! Linnea acknowledged the presence of her dog. I was beginning to think Autumn was a fabrication.

I'd been sitting still too long. Again I had an unsettling, disoriented feeling. I knew I was on my own porch. Those were my own dogs grouped around me; that was the yellow Victorian across the lane, all anchoring me to the present time.

But was there a wayward chill in the air? If I blinked my eye, would it start snowing?

No, I was nowhere near Huron Court and thankful for that.

Once again, I reflected on how different Linnea's experience was from mine. I had never left the vicinity of Huron Court. It had never occurred to me to go exploring. If it had, would I have been able to visit my own past?

I didn't want to do that, wasn't the least bit interested in altering what had gone before. I wondered again exactly what Linnea wished to change and if she were aware of the different path that change might set her on.

For example, if she were successful, she wouldn't have come to Lucy and me for help. I would never have heard of a lost collie named Autumn. This journal I was reading wouldn't exist.

It was all too confusing to contemplate on a peaceful summer day. I left the journal on the porch table and went inside out of the heat before the sun could scramble my brain.

Ten

Linnea and I had arranged to meet at Clovers at eleven-thirty on Wednesday. Thanks to a series of domestic and canine interruptions, I hadn't finished reading the journal, but I didn't think it would matter. The basic plot would remain unchanged.

I arrived early and sat at my favorite booth, contemplating the view of the Crispian Road woods. They were still green with only the faintest hints of yellow and red. Summer was still firmly entrenched in Foxglove Corners.

Linnea was late. A few minutes, then twenty, then a half hour. I ordered a lime cooler and felt my patience rapidly slipping away. I hate waiting, especially when I suspect that a person won't show up.

But the lunch date was Linnea's idea. I had chosen the place, Clovers, and she had suggested the day and time. When an entire hour had gone by with no sign of her and no call, I decided I was going to have to eat alone.

Annica hovered over me with her order pad and pen. "Do you think she stood you up?"

"It looks that way," I said. "I'm going to go ahead and order."

"The special is good."

A bowl of split pea soup and a ham salad sandwich. I placed my order and Annica passed it to her fellow waitress, Marcy. She sat with me, declaring it was time for her break.

"That lady is incredibly rude," Annica said. "She could have let you know if something came up."

"Or she may have been prevented from joining me."

"By what?"

"An accident? She may still call."

I didn't really believe that.

"From what you've told me, she sounds like she's off her rocker," Annica said. "From now on, don't have anything to do with her."

"But there's her lost collie to consider."

"Who's to say she even has a dog?"

I'd wondered that myself. There was so much about the situation I didn't know.

"I wouldn't be so quick to trust her." Annica touched her enamel earring, a miniature slice of watermelon, as if to make sure it was still there. "Can we talk about my problem for a minute?"

This was the first indication that all was not well in her world. Even in a hot pink dress, her radiance seemed a trifle subdued.

"What's wrong?" I asked.

"Nothing yet, but that red-headed witch is having a party for the Hunt Club next week."

"The red-headed witch being Alethea Venn, I assume."

"None other. It's going to be a gala affair. Brent asked me to go with him."

"Don't you want to go?"

"I'm afraid she's planning to do something to undermine our relationship."

Ah! The heart of the matter. I could sympathize. Once a female deputy sheriff, Veronica, had set her sights on my husband, Crane, knowing full well he was married. I'd nicknamed her the Viper.

"What can Alethea do?" I asked. "Brent has made his choice. You have a gorgeous engagement ring to prove it."

"Alethea doesn't like me."

"That's beside the point. She considers Brent her property. She doesn't want him, but she doesn't want you to have him either. All she can do is ignore you."

"I'm expecting that. It's what she always does."

"Did you tell Brent how you feel?" I asked.

"No. He's looking forward to it. Those Hunt Club people are his friends."

"And you're his *fiancée*."

I didn't know what else I could say. Usually Annica had a surplus of self-confidence. But Alethea was her Waterloo.

I would like nothing better than to see Alethea defeated in her own war. But I wasn't on her invitation list, nor would I want to be. All I could do was offer Annica my advice and wishes for a happy evening.

"I want to do everything right," she said.

"Just be yourself. Buy a great new dress if you think it'll help. Plan to have fun. It'll be a night out with Brent, and, as you say, a gala one."

"I guess," she said.

~ * ~

Once I was home, my annoyance at Linnea's cavalier treatment of me faded to curiosity, but not the kind that has to be satisfied immediately. I had plenty to do and eight collies to take care of, although, in truth, they were adept at taking care of themselves. It was too hot for long walks, and playtime turned into snooze time. Dinner was taken care of. Crane was going to barbecue chicken; I'd made a pasta salad and brought a strawberry pie from Clovers for dessert.

During an afternoon lull, I decided to call Linnea. I deserved an explanation and wondered once again about Autumn. Was Linnea sincere in wanting my help?

At my desk, I searched the 'W' section in my address book for Linnea's contact information. I had it all: land line and cell phone numbers and e-mail address.

It wasn't there.

It had to be.

I turned back to 'V,' then forward to 'X.' Both pages were blank. I turned to 'W' again. There was no entry for Linnea Wilmott.

Although there had to be. I remembered copying it from a Post-it note Linnea had given me. Just before taking Sky, Star, and Gemmy for their afternoon walk. Then, of course, I'd thrown the note away, probably torn it into pieces.

Surely I couldn't have imagined it. Or dreamed it. No phantom had invaded my home to tear a page from my address book.

My frantic thoughts flew in every direction. I went through the entire address book, through every section, every entry, always expecting to find the missing information recorded in the wrong place.

Finally I had to admit the truth. It wasn't there, and I couldn't explain what had happened—or more accurately—hadn't happened.

Eventually I set the matter aside, consigning it to Saint Anthony, patron of all things lost.

What else could I do?

A possible answer occurred to me later as I discussed the day's strangeness with Crane.

Somehow Linnea had traveled back in time and changed her past. She hadn't lost Autumn. She'd never shared her story with Lucy and me. She hadn't begged me to help her.

She'd never given me her contact information, so I'd never copied it into my address book.

That was a more satisfying explanation than admitting I'd lost my grip on reality.

Eleven

"It's weird," I told Crane after dinner as I outlined my time change theory. "An entire incident has been erased from my life."

Crane folded the *Banner* and drained the last of his coffee. "There must be a simpler explanation."

"Such as?"

"Sometimes you take multi-tasking too far. You may have thought you copied Linnea's number. You meant to."

"But suddenly I was distracted and didn't go back to what I was doing. I'll take it. Only..."

"What?"

"Then where's Linnea's Post-It note? When I didn't find her number in my address book, I dumped the contents of my purse out on the desk looking for it. No surprise. It wasn't there."

"You'll have to wait for Linnea to get in touch with you," Crane said. "The ball's in her court."

I sat back and reviewed my 'butterfly effect' explanation, immediately seeing a way to test it. Lucy was my witness.

Now, if Lucy claimed that Linnea never told us about her experience on Huron Court...Wait! I had another piece of evidence.

Linnea's journal. It was where I'd left it, on the side table next to the rocker.

I had her story written in indelible blue ink. It did happen.

"I'm going to run this by Lucy," I said. "Maybe she's heard from Linnea."

In the meantime, I reached for the journal. I'd left Linnea in front of her family home about to look for a dog friendly motel. What happened next?

~ * ~

LINNEA'S JOURNAL

I left the house with the greatest reluctance. In spite of being lost in time, it was the only home I had in this insane world. But I couldn't shelter within its walls. For me, who was also lost in time, it was a shadow of the past, appearing real but without substance.

I was…I didn't know what I was.

Tired, confused, hungry, cold…

Why cold? The heater was working. My borrowed parka was warm.

As I drove down Main Street searching for a motel, I noticed a drive-in restaurant, vaguely remembered from my college days, long out of business. Here I ordered two hamburgers, one plain for Autumn, one with relish for me, and we ate them in the car.

Food gave me a much-needed boost, and when I saw the Royal Motel on the outskirts of town, I told Autumn to lie on the floor and didn't mention that I had a dog with me. The manager, more interested in his coffee and newspaper than his customer, didn't notice that I wasn't alone.

The room was depressing, small with a double bed that swallowed up most of the space, a nightstand, and a television. The color scheme was a dispirited mix of earth tones, with a lone landscape, a sunbaked desert scene on the wall, and the bathroom was so tiny I could scarcely turn around in it.

But it was warm, a port of sorts in the storm. I spilled out the contents of my purse on the bed. When I left home this morning for a drive in the country, who knew my supplies would have to last for an indefinite period? Maybe for the rest of my life.

I had forty dollars in cash and credit cards that were worthless in 1998, together with a handful of change, a hairbrush, a cosmetic bag, and an empty pill box. I also had a small pad of Post-It notes and a red pen.

With only these homely items and a car, I had to face a world that was wholly alien. One that didn't exist. Even though it did. The very idea of time travel could tie me up in knots I had no hope of undoing.

I washed my face and lay on top of the bed, planning to watch the late news and track the snowstorm.

Autumn jumped up beside me, scratched at the spread, and curled into a ball. She had no worries; I was in charge. I let my hand rest on her head. My sweet Autumn collie. I wasn't alone.

That was my last memory of the most terrifying day of my life.

I woke with one clear thought: It didn't happen. It was only a horrible dream. I would open the door and summer would be back in all its glory. Sunshine, warmth, flowers blooming on the roadside. What an adventure I'd had!

Only why was I in this drab room instead of my own bedroom?

Images from yesterday returned in a flood, threatening to overwhelm me. Somehow I had been snatched away from my proper time and dumped in the past on a snowy winter day. This was 1998. A glance out the window confirmed the grim reality. Everything in my view was buried in a major snowfall. It was early, six-thirty by my watch.

I had to leave the motel quickly before the manager saw Autumn. And go where? Back home? My home in the past?

Somehow I had to reverse what had happened, and if I had any hope of doing this, I needed to go back to where it started, with an ill-fated turn on Huron Court.

It felt good to have a plan.

I pulled my jeans and sleeveless top back on and added the ugly parka. Taking my purse, I led Autumn out to the lot where she immediately squatted in the pristine snow.

Thankfully no one was around to observe us. I had to admit this unwelcome world looked appealing with fresh snow glistening in the weak early light. The plows hadn't been out yet.

It didn't matter. I had a half tank of gas, and the street was all but deserted, the roads clear of traffic for the most part. There was no one to notice a car that hadn't been built yet. No one to care.

Once again, I headed out of town—north to Foxglove Corners and Huron Court while the snow began to fall.

Twelve

Linnea's Journal-resumes

Few people were out and about this morning, which resulted in an easy drive and time to think about the many problems I would face if I didn't return to my own year.

In the present, my present, that is, I had plenty of money in my checking account, while in 1998 I hadn't begun to save regularly and didn't have a credit card. My emergency money was in a drawer in a house that hadn't been built yet. All I had in my wallet was forty dollars. No, less than that after paying for the motel and last night's dinner.

And what about breakfast? I was already hungry, and I'd have to buy food for Autumn and a dish. I'd only brought a bag of treats and a small bowl for water, supplies adequate for a day trip.

I had a sudden craving for doughnuts fresh from the oven. Cinnamon, pumpkin, powdered, glazed, any kind would do.

Warm clothes were a necessity. Before long, my forty dollars would be gone. In fact, I doubted I could buy a pair of wool slacks and a sweater for what remained in my wallet. Then what would I do for food? My mind leaped ahead to the future, that is to my own time.

What would the principal think when I didn't show up for my classes after the Christmas vacation? Fortunately, I had a few days' grace before school resumed. So much could happen in those few days.

Would anyone miss me? I had friends, but we weren't in constant contact. We didn't keep one another informed of our comings and goings.

I would be one of those unfortunate souls who vanish into the thin air, along with her car and her dog, never to be seen again.

I felt cold in spite of the heater. What if I couldn't find the way back to my own time? It wasn't as if I had a road map.

I kept driving and telling myself that I would be home soon, maybe before dark. Somehow. Perhaps as easily as I'd slid into the past. Perhaps any minute now.

The snow continued to fall lightly, steadily. I was on the same road I'd taken yesterday, but everything looked different.

In the years to come, new houses would be added to the landscape, whole blocks of the large mansions that had become so popular. The little town that loomed ahead, known as Groversville, and scarcely deserving of the designation 'town,' would grow to contain a Main Street with stores. That was far in the future, though. Too many years.

After I passed Groversville, the view was increasingly wild with woods draped in snow and icy lakes. Soon I would reach Huron Court and maybe this time, it would prove to be the road home.

As I turned on Huron Court, I said a short prayer to the keepers of Time, willing them to work their magic and take me home.

Nothing happened.

Only yesterday bright wildflowers had sparkled along the roadside. Were they still there, buried under the impossible snowfall? It seemed to be tapering off. Or was that wishful thinking?

Then I saw a magnificent pink Victorian house behind a mist of snow, bright with outdoor lights shining on turrets and gables. It looked like a fairy tale castle shimmering in a winter wonderland.

Why hadn't I seen it yesterday?

For a split second, I took my eyes off the road. The car skidded on hidden ice, doing a crazy dance across the narrow lanes. My heart doing its own crazy dance, I stepped hard on the brake, definitely the wrong move, and came to rest against a large bush. The motor died.

I felt a sharp pain in my neck and shoulder, felt like an object dropped into a blender and tossed about. Autumn gave a high-pitched yelp and started to cry.

Luckily, it appeared the car had escaped damage, thanks to the bush. I freed myself from the seat belt, opened the door, and sank deep in snow, forgetting I wasn't wearing boots. Yes, a quick look told me the car was all right.

Thunder crashed above my head. Autumn pushed past me. I shouted her name and reached for her collar. Too late. Panicked by the storm, she ran. I was left grasping air, more confused than ever.

Thunder in a snowstorm?

It was rare but not impossible.

The sight that met my eyes, however, simply couldn't be.

The pink Victorian house had vanished. In its place, a vast snow-covered field rolled away to a dark wood, suddenly illuminated by a flash of lightning.

Warm raindrops fell on my face. All around me the snow began to melt. The air grew heavy and humid, and the flowers were back. You would think it would take a long time for so much snow to melt, but the transformation was practically instantaneous.

That meant it was no longer winter. No longer 1998. To be certain, I would have to backtrack and find a store or restaurant with another newspaper. Better still, I could turn on the radio.

Maybe it was all a dream, after all, but it had seemed so real...My voice shook as I called Autumn. "Come, girl! Hurry! We're leaving."

There was no answering bark, only the sounds of birdsong carried on the wind.

Thirteen

"The journal ends there," I said to Annica the next day as we lingered over a late lunch at Clovers. "There are about ten pages left. All blank."

Annica glanced at her empty glass as if wondering how her lime cooler could have miraculously evaporated. "There may be another journal."

"I don't think so. Linnea's story came to an end with the thunderstorm that melted the snow and brought her back to her own time. Once she was safe, it must have occurred her to that she could make certain changes in her life if she'd stayed in the past. She spent all summer trying to return to the past."

"May I read the journal?" Annica asked.

"I don't think she'd mind. It reads like a thrilling science-fiction story—without a proper end."

"If I were planning a time trip, I'd take plenty of money and pack clothes for any season," Annica said. "And medicine and my earrings..."

She drifted off, perhaps realizing that she might not have a chance to take her favorite things along.

"Well, Linnea didn't plan this one," I said. "I can see why she thinks she lost Autumn in the past, but it might have happened in the present. In our time, that is. Autumn ran away during the thunderstorm—between time."

"Between time," Annica murmured. "Weird. We'll never find her."

"I'm wondering if we'll find Linnea."

"That would be something, to find the dog but not the owner," Annica said. "What's our next step?"

"After lunch I'm going to see Lucy. Then I think we'll pick up the trail on Huron Court. Whether in the past or present, that's where Autumn was last seen—at the wildflower field but several years before the pink Victorian burned."

"Are we looking for Linnea or Autumn?" Annica asked.

"Both."

I scanned the handwritten menu propped up in front of the sugar bowl, wondering if Clovers had been in existence in 1998.

"Weren't you afraid to drive on Huron Court?" Annica asked.

"Alone, yes. Can you go with me?"

"If we can make it tomorrow early. I have a noon class. But I can't imagine what we'll find."

"We have no other place to look," I said. "Maybe Lucy will have some ideas."

~ * ~

Lucy set a plate of chocolate wafers on the coffee table and gave Sky a biscuit. The gold Zodiak charms on her bracelet jingled, a merry contrast to the grim subject of our discussion.

"Linnea didn't erase herself from life's canvas, Jennet," Lucy said. "I saw her write her information on a Post-It note and give it to you. She's still around in the here and now, but I don't know where."

The blank space in my address book was destined to remain a mystery then.

"Doesn't she call you?" I asked.

"Not often. Usually if she wants my input on a plot point."

"She doesn't answer when I call her."

Linnea Wilmott wasn't the first person of my acquaintance to drop out of sight. Often it meant the missing one had run into trouble. With Linnea, I didn't know what to think.

"She'll get in touch with you if she needs you," Lucy said. "Otherwise, she's something of a recluse."

"I wonder if she found her way back to 1998."

"That was her goal, but who knows? Let's see what the tea leaves will reveal."

Lucy often cautioned me to take her readings with a grain of salt. I did, but also remembered how many times her warnings had alerted me to danger in time to forearm myself.

One more swallow. I drained the excess tea into the saucer and turned the cup toward me three times while making a wish, this time that I would be able to help Linnea find Autumn, which was two wishes, now that I thought of it.

Lucy took the cup from me and promptly said, "I see a dog."

She pointed to a leaf that did indeed resemble a very tiny collie silhouette—if you enlisted the power of imagination.

"And uh-oh. This isn't good. I see danger. Here's a curving path with a monstrous thing lying in wait for you. Here you are." She pointed to a straight leaf midway down the side of the cup. It was lighter than its fellows.

"Is that Huron Court?" I asked.

"There's no road sign in a teacup, but that would be my guess."

"Can you be more specific? 'Thing' is rather vague."

"It's monstrous," Lucy said. "And it's determined."

"Is it human?"

"I think so."

"I'm searching for a lost dog," I said. "How can that be dangerous?"

Lucy shrugged. "It depends where the dog leads you."

I imagined rounding a curve on Huron Court and driving into a snowstorm and into another time. How far was I willing to follow Autumn, assuming I managed to find her?

Not that far.

And—logistics reared its head—how could I transport her back to the present? Just attach her collar to her leash and drag her along through the decades? Well, no use wondering. As I'd told Linnea, I didn't plan to get swept up in the time winds.

"Linnea is the one who wants to revisit the past," I said. "I'm happy with my life. I've never been happier."

"Shh." Lucy glanced over her shoulder, and even Sky looked wary. "Don't tempt fate. I don't see your wish," she added.

Well, darn. Did that mean I wasn't going to reunite Linnea and Autumn?

Remember the grain of salt, I told myself.

Fourteen

It wouldn't be a genuine adventure without Lucy's pronouncements of gloom and doom. I wasn't overly concerned about the human menace, though, as this adventure didn't contain any villains. None that I knew of, that is.

At home, I realized I couldn't do anything to advance the mystery today. Nor did I want to. I needed to think about what to make for dinner and regroup.

Leaving further developments for the future, I turned my attention to my collies. They'd all sought out their favorite resting places on the first floor. Some were sleeping or gnawing on a chew toy. Others watched me, hoping I'd say or do something to break the monotony.

"Who wants to go for a walk?" I asked.

Misty, Gemmy, and Halley looked up. Gemmy stretched and ambled to the door while Misty stationed herself at my side. I knew exactly where we'd go—to nearby Sagramore Lake, the best place to while away a sweltering summer afternoon.

I leashed them, and we plowed through the heat to the beach. With the delicious scent of water riding on the air, the temperature seemed cooler, practically balmy. Soon we were halfway down Sagramore Lake Road, and I imagined I felt the light caress of lake spray on my arms.

God bless our Michigan lakes.

Two girls and a collie were running on the beach, the girls' bright yellow tops a burst of color in a blue sky-and-sand landscape. Molly and Jennifer, my young friends who lived on Sagramore Lake Road, waved when they spied us, and collie Ginger barked out her welcome.

The girls looked like sisters, dressed alike with glowing faces and long ponytails. As they came to a stop, I read the logo on their tops: Dogfinders, Inc.

"Is that a new organization?" I asked. "I've never heard of it."

"It's our organization," Jennifer said. "We recruited a group of people to find lost dogs. Some are kids from our school, but we have adult members too. As soon as a dog goes missing, we work as a team and go into action."

"We're all volunteers," Molly added. "If there's a reward, it goes straight into our fund."

"We got the idea when Rainbow was stolen," Jennifer said.

She referred to the collie who had been snatched from her crate at the Collie Walkathon earlier this summer.

"A lost dog's chances of being found increase when a lot of people are looking for him," Jennifer pointed out.

"What exactly do you do?" I asked.

"The same as any owner would, but there are more of us, twenty as of last week. We put up posters and look everywhere, and we don't stop until we find him. One of our people has a radio show in Lakeville."

Naturally I thought of Autumn.

"As it happens, I know of a missing collie," I said. "Will you be on the lookout for a sable and white female? She's about three, and her name is Autumn."

"Do you have a picture of her?" Molly asked.

"No. I might be able to get one."

But could I? I couldn't even locate Linnea.

"That'll help," Molly said. "Do you know how she got lost?"

I paused to think, not prepared to answer questions in detail. "She was frightened by thunder and bolted."

That was true. I saw no need to add that this might have happened in another time.

"Where did this happen?"

I didn't want to mention Huron Court, didn't want the girls to go anywhere near that nefarious roadway lest they fall prey to its proclivities.

On the other hand, how likely was it that Autumn would stay there?

Very likely, I thought on reflection. It was the last place she'd seen her mistress. But no one could know for certain where a lost dog would end up. And what if Linnea was right, and she was still in 1998?

Again I gave a partial answer. "In Foxglove Corners. Probably nearby."

"We usually interview the owners," Jennifer said. "Can you put us in touch with Autumn's family?"

"Not at this time. If you stop by in a day or two, I may be able to give you more information."

Or so I hoped.

"Okay then. We'll alert everyone to look for a sable female collie," Molly said. "So far, we have a perfect record."

I prayed Autumn wouldn't turn out to be the exception.

~ * ~

At home, three exhausted collies fell on their water bowls, drank their fill, and settled down for an after-walk nap. I glanced at the unwieldy mound of mail on the kitchen table and decided to weed out the junk.

Mixed in with catalogues and advertisements was a letter addressed to me in an unfamiliar hand. I opened the envelope to find a single sheet of paper folded around a smaller envelope addressed to Miss Jennet Greenway at my old Oakpoint address. Smudged and wrinkled, it looked as if it had been sent ages ago and bandied about in a storm. A stamp indicated that the item was undeliverable, and beneath, someone had added my correct name and current address.

The handwriting looked familiar. I'd just spent hours looking at it in a journal. However unlikely it seemed, apparently I was holding a message from Linnea Wilmot.

Not bothering to look for a letter opener, I tore the envelope open and read:

Dear Jennet,

As you can see, my efforts paid off. I made it back to the past, but I'm in 2015, years ahead of where I wanted to be. You were right. Time is unpredictable. Now I need help. Please go to 316 Willow Avenue in Lakeville. I left something for you in the garden under an angel statue. Hoping it's still there and hope to see you soon.

Linnea Wilmott

In 2015? I didn't think so.

I then read the paragraph on the enclosed paper:

With apologies for the long delay, this letter turned up in our facility last week. No one can explain how it came to be overlooked all this time. I'm sending it on to you and hope it's still relevant. Leigh Grace

How weird to hold a letter from the past in my hand, a message from Linnea Wilmott. Weird but welcome. What I had was my first real clue, a solid lead to follow.

But something buried under an angel statue? How bizarre.

And how in the name of everything that's holy could I use whatever it was to help Linnea?

Fifteen

I set the letter aside, unable to concentrate on making dinner. A memory had just surfaced: Crane and I on Huron Court hearing the hum of an engine summarily cut off. The absence of any other vehicle on the road. A minor mystery unsolved. How could I have forgotten?

Could we have heard Linnea's car as she drove into the past to a year arbitrarily chosen by whatever entity managed the time on that rogue roadway?

Maybe. Or maybe some other unlucky traveler had been whisked away to another year. It appeared that Huron Court was ready to erupt any moment like a restless volcano.

With that in mind, I reconsidered my plan to search the area for Autumn. What I could do, however, was drive to Lakeville and see what Linnea had left for me under the angel statue. That, at least, was perfectly safe.

"Don't count on finding anything," Crane said when I shared the latest developments with him later that day. "It was a long time ago. Things change."

He could be more encouraging. "I can't ignore a clue," I said.

"I just don't want you to be disappointed."

"I won't be. This is a mystery like none other. I'm expecting roadblocks."

"I know the neighborhood," Crane said. "There's a lot of building going on. They tear down perfectly good houses and replace them with big flashy ones. And if the house is still there, you can't break into someone's backyard and fool around with their lawn decoration."

"We'll see."

"We?"

"Annica will want to go with me. She doesn't like to be left out of a mystery."

"Have you tried to get in touch with Linnea—in this timeline?" he asked.

"I've called her a few times. She doesn't answer."

Was she still in 2015? I thought so. If she had returned to our time, surely she would have contacted me. Her silence told me she was still in the past, stranded in the wrong year and in some unspecified trouble. Waiting for me to help her.

In 2015? I didn't think so.

But assuming her goal was to change her past, couldn't she still do that in 2015? She was only seven years from her intended destination.

These last days of summer vacation would have been so much more peaceful if I'd never met Linnea Willmott, if I could travel back in time myself and not accept Lucy's tea party invitation.

Oh well, I might as well enjoy the challenge of a new mystery before heading back to classrooms, schoolwork, and unfamiliar faces.

If only this one weren't all wrapped up in the mysterious strands of time.

~ * ~

At the end of her shift at Clovers, Annica joined me for a lime cooler. She was eager to take part in the search for Linnea's time capsule, as she referred to it.

"Tonight is Alethea's party," she said. "I've been worrying about it non-stop so I'll welcome a distraction."

She appeared to have forgotten the pep talk I'd given her. I'd have to reinforce it.

"You'll be fine," I promised her. "We can have lunch in Lakeville and maybe visit the Green House of Antiques."

"Are you going to take a shovel?" she asked.

"Goodness, no. I can't dig in someone else's yard."

"What'll we do then?"

"Play it by ear. If the statue's there, we'll lift it."

"What if it's life-sized?"

"I'm picturing a small garden figurine. Linnea had to be able to manage it by herself."

"It's the oddest way of communication," she said. "I wonder what she left for you?"

"A map? A key? Another letter? It could be anything."

I wondered, too. Instead of trying to contact me in this bizarre fashion, why hadn't Linnea simply driven back to Huron Court and tried to travel to another year? Ideally, back to the present.

One reason occurred to me: the road wouldn't let her return to the present. If she were in 2015, she couldn't even look for Autumn.

"The weirdest things have been happening lately," Annica said. "How do you think the letter got lost?"

"It fell behind a counter or something. I read about a letter written after World War Two that lay hidden for decades. It reunited two people who thought they'd lost contact forever and inspired a made-for-television movie."

"And why did she send it to a house you haven't lived in for years?"

"The house on Jonquil Lane may not have been built yet. At any rate, I wasn't living in Foxglove Corners then."

I became aware of a light jab above my right eye. I hoped it wasn't the beginning of a headache, as my day was packed with a full array of everyday chores along with this unique quest. I wanted to be in good shape to make the most of it.

~ * ~

The sun was hot as we strolled down Willow Avenue, doing our best to look as if we belonged in the neighborhood. Crane was right. Every fifth house was one of those gaudy McMansions too large for its lot and too fancy for the neat brick ranches that filled the rest of the block.

It was quiet with no one around, not even children, which suited us, and 316 Willow had a 'For Sale' sign in the front yard. We stood in front of the house as if admiring its features and gradually edged around to the back yard.

The sweet scent of recently mowed grass lingered in the air and neat beds set off by colorful rocks contained well cared-for flowers. They looked as if they'd just been planted, and the red mulch was fresh. I didn't see any statuary, not even a bird bath.

"We're too late," I said. "The yard is staged to appeal to buyers. New owners can add their own decorations. Who knows what happened to the angel statue? It could be anywhere. Maybe someone got rid of it."

Annica peered behind a leafy bush and shook her head. "Nothing. Like I said, it was a weird way of communicating with you."

I had assured Crane that I was expecting a roadblock but had to admit I was disappointed. If this were a mystery story instead of real life, we would have unearthed the statue and have its secret in our possession now. What if it were another journal?

A curtain in the second story room of the house next door was pulled back, then dropped into place.

"Did you see that?" Annica asked. "We'd better move on before the neighbor calls the police."

"I'm not worried. The house is for sale. We're buyers checking out the yard."

But I agreed with her. Linnea's time capsule, if it still existed, was beyond our reach, our first real lead gone before we had a chance to find it. We could only hope to find another. It was time to move on.

"Time for lunch," Annica announced.

Sixteen

After a lunch of tuna salad sandwiches, Annica and I wandered down Antique Row, stopping to admire the window display at the Green House of Antiques before going inside.

The summertime beach theme had given way to a fall scene of scattered books on a carpet of russet leaves. Two mannequins clad in period dress sat in mini replicas of school desks, imparting a somber message: Summer is winding down. School is waiting. Farewell to carefree August days. A message on a playschool-sized blackboard announced a summer sale.

Small brass bells rang out a welcome as I opened the door. A scent of lavender drifted over us, a fragrance new to my experience in the Green House. Perhaps a half dozen customers quietly examined the various pieces of furniture and accessories set out to lure the customer into a peaceful, more gracious world.

Lola, a saleswoman known to me from countless visits to the shop, paused in the act of rearranging plates on a table set with autumn-themed china. She wore a glittering flapper's dress with beads that dropped to her waist and a bejeweled band holding back her wavy dark hair.

"I know what you ladies like." She had a smile for each one of us. "Books in a series and vintage jewelry. We have some lovely earrings on sale, and I just set out a shipment of new books. Old books, that is."

"It's lucky we stopped in today," I said.

Annica lost no time in gravitating toward a sales table covered with jewelry and Tiffany lamps.

I paused to admire the autumnal china, then reminded myself that I had three complete sets of dishes already and only used one of them. I moved farther into the shop, following the fragrance of lavender.

Usually, vintage books were displayed throughout the store on tables or nightstands as they would be in a private home. Today I saw a small narrow bookcase painted white and decorated with gingerbread trim. On its top a pitcher held a bunch of deep blue hydrangeas, and its shelves were full. It stood by itself between two velvet chairs, also blue.

I moved to it as if drawn by a magical cord. This was my passion. Books with timeworn covers, some with slightly tattered dust jackets. Yellowing pages. Glorious illustrations. *The Bobbsey Twins in the Country*, an early edition based on the charming cover art depicting Flossie and Freddie in a flowering meadow.

I scanned the titles, hoping to find a Judy Bolton or Beverly Grey to add to my collection, but the selection seemed to belong to an earlier time than the days of Judy and Beverly.

A title on the middle shelf practically leaped out at me. *Linda Welsch and the Time Machine*. I'd never heard of Linda Welsch and, having limited my collection to mysteries, never come across a science-fiction book with a female protagonist. This was a rare treasure.

And a strange one. My collection wasn't extensive, but over the years I had researched the names of American series and their authors and had a reasonable amount of knowledge to fall back on. Why had I never come across Linda Welsch?

The cover intrigued me. A girl in turn-of-the-(last)-century garb with streaming yellow hair floated in mid-air above an apparatus that resembled an early television set.

The author was June Summers—most likely a penname—and the copyright date was 1911. This particular volume had been a birthday present to 'Miss Catherine Elizabeth.' According to a page at the end of the book, it was the first in a new series. The second book was *Linda Welsch in the Wild West*.

Who, I wondered, was Linda Welsch? I'd have to buy the book to find out, which would be no hardship. I tucked it under my arm and examined the shelves to see if I could find the second book, but apparently the store had only the first.

Annica came up behind me. "Did you find something?"

"Just one book," I said," but it's something special."

She held a spray of tiny green stones and pearls held together with a brushed silver ribbon. "I found these. Aren't they beautiful?"

"Exquisite. Will you wear them tonight?"

"Oh, no, I'm wearing the emeralds Brent gave me for Christmas. I'll be wearing these for every day."

"How many pairs of earrings do you have?" I asked.

"I stopped counting them years ago."

I nodded. "I stopped counting my books, too, but this one is different. I can't wait to read it. I just wish I had more space."

I considered. Maybe I should buy the pretty white bookcase or at least ask Lola how much it was. I could see it in a corner of our bedroom topped with a vase of flowers from our garden. I would keep my favorite books in it.

Our pleasant lunch and my new acquisition had restored my optimistic mood, and as I walked to the cash register, I felt somehow compensated for not finding the angel statue and the secret it guarded.

~ * ~

Annica helped me carry my new bookcase into the house whereupon the dogs gathered around it sniffing, detecting the scents of the past or the whiff of lavender that clung to it, albeit subtly.

I ran my fingers along the scrolled decoration above the top shelf. "This wasn't made in a factory."

"I wish Lola could have told us its history," Annica said. "In her place I would have, or made one up."

When I'd first met Annica she'd been working in an antique shop, Past Perfect. For every item she hoped to sell, she had a tale, usually macabre, guaranteed to arouse a buyer's interest.

I put my Linda Welsch book on the coffee table. "Would you like a drink, Annica? I have fresh lemonade."

"I'd love one, but I have to get ready for tonight."

"It's only four o'clock."

"Everything has to be perfect, and perfection takes time."

"Relax and have fun at the party," I said.

"That's a tall order."

I understood. I would much rather stay home in my beloved Victorian farmhouse than socialize with the dreadful Alethea Venn and her arrogant Hunt Club friends. Excepting Brent Fowler.

The rest of the afternoon was relatively easy. Take care of the dogs, play with them, make a salad. Crane was grilling chicken, so I didn't have to cook dinner. I lugged my new bookcase up the stairs to our bedroom and hunted for a vase like the one I'd seen at the Green House.

That done, my new book called to me, urging me to sink into the rocker and read, read, read.

But a pleasure delayed is twice as enjoyable. Also I wanted to read the entire book in one sitting.

"Later," I said and gathered the ingredients for my salad.

Seventeen

Linda Welsch was the only daughter of an eminent scientist. They lived in a stately old house in a small Michigan town named Pinecrest. Linda's father taught at the university while she attended the local high school where she was in her senior year.

Linda whiled away her days with drives in the country and picnics on the lake with Annie and Stella, referred to as chums. She had a boyfriend, Rob, and a dog named Shady, whose description brought to mind an old-fashioned collie. In her free time, she helped her father in his home laboratory, which is how she became aware of the marvelous new machine he was building.

Michigan...a collie...drives in the countryside...As I turned the fragile pages, an idea flickered in my mind and gradually took shape. A wild, fantastic idea that was, somehow, barely possible. Could June Summers possibly be the missing Linnea Wilmott?

Was it really so far-fetched? Linnea had traveled to 2015 long enough to leave something for me under a lawn ornament. I assumed she was trying desperately to get home, only to land in the wrong year, time and time again.

And would she have stayed in the early years of the nineteenth century long enough to write a book and have it published? It would be a way to earn a modest income and perhaps send another message, perhaps letting a future reader know what had become of her. She was, after all, a writer in her current life.

If that were the case, she must have stayed in that arbitrary year for some time and might possibly still be there.

What was Huron Court like in, say, 1910? My house and most of the others in the vicinity wouldn't have been built. The land was a virtual wilderness, and apparently Huron Court's ability to send travelers to another time was more powerful.

The need for an income made more sense than a message. How could Linnea know I would find her book in an antique shop? It didn't seem likely, but once the idea took hold, I found myself looking for evidence that Linnea Wilmott and June Summers were one and the same.

Linda's father had invented a hand-held telephone that enabled people to see one another on a tiny screen. He designed a miniature stove that could heat a plate of leftovers in seconds and even cook a meal. He altered the family automobile so it could be activated and driven with the push of a button.

Linda didn't use any of these marvels in her daily life but mentioned them.

The story was simple. One day, by accident, Linda sent herself soaring into a future age when the earth was a desert broiling under an angry sun. She thought herself alone in this alien world until she encountered three hostile members of a race that lived mostly in underground cities. As she was on the verge of being captured, her father somehow brought her back home.

Deus ex machina. The author was skimpy on scientific details but generous with action.

The book ended with a preview of Linda's next adventure when she set out on a vacation in the West with her chums. The girls wound up in Colorado Territory in 1866. The brief summary didn't mention what part the time machine played in that particular trip.

By now, I was thoroughly invested in Linda's life and wished I could read the second book without the requisite search. I was determined to find it. If it existed.

But first I needed to call Linnea's number again. If she were in our time, if she answered, I'd have a quick answer. If not...

~ * ~

She didn't answer. I hadn't expected her to, but one of my mottos being 'leave no stone unturned,' I left yet another message on her voice mail. Next I called Lucy.

"Did you ever hear from Linnea Wilmott?" I asked.

"Not a word. As I told you, she'll make contact with us when she needs something."

"She may have already done that. Are you busy? I need to run something by you in person."

"Come over anytime," Lucy said. "I'll admit I'm curious."

An hour later, Lucy and I were drinking tea in her sunroom, the Linda Welsch book lying on the wicker coffee table in front of us. Sky, sitting next to me, was inordinately interested in it, as my collies had been in the bookcase from the Green House. Could she detect Linnea's scent on the book, assuming this had been Linnea's personal copy? Could a dog's sense possibly be that powerful?

I thought it unlikely. An item that had been stored in an antique shop would have acquired thousands of enticing scents to delight the nose of a collie.

Lucy had listened to my theory and skimmed through the book.

"Did you search for the series on the Internet?" she asked.

I'd done that before calling Lucy.

"Yes, and I also looked on eBay and Esty and posted queries on old series sites. It seems no one has heard of Linda Welsch."

"L. W. and L. W. A coincidence? That second title may not have been written or published. What do they call those unborn books? Phantoms?"

"I like 'unborn' better," I said. "I couldn't find any mention of June Summers either."

"I don't know what to say, Jennet," Lucy said. "Your idea seems way, way out in left field, but it's possible. We know Linnea time traveled once. It's possible that she did it again and again and ended up in two wrong times."

"When it happened to me, I never left Huron Court," I said, "and it seemed like forever, but it wasn't that long. Certainly not long enough to settle down in another time and write a book."

The experiences of Brent and Annica had been similar to mine. Into the past and back to the future after a brief but frightening time.

I took a sip of tea. I'd been talking so much my throat had grown dry. "Did Linnea ever tell you what she wanted to change about her past?"

"Not specifically, but she implied it concerned a man. She thought if she'd done something different, he would be a part of her life now, and she wanted that very much."

"Now," I murmured. "Now is relative. If Linnea is in the wrong time, it won't happen. And where does that leave Autumn?"

How easy to forget that a lost collie was a part of this wild, improbable tale.

"I wish Linnea could find her way home." I glanced at the book. "Maybe I'm wrong and June Summers is someone else. Do you have Linnea's address?"

"Yes, in my book. Why?"

"I'd like to see her house. Maybe she's been there all along but doesn't want to communicate with us. In which case, this is the only book in an obscure series."

"I'll go with you," Lucy said.

Eighteen

As I turned on the street where Linnea lived, I thought about Autumn. She, too, had lost her home, and possibly her owner. I was honor-bound to do all in my power to find her, and if Linnea stayed in the past, Sue Appleton would find her a new family. Assuming Autumn had gone missing in my time, that is.

"We have to find Autumn," I told Lucy. "Molly and Jennifer and their new group of volunteers will help. They call themselves Dogfinders, Inc."

"I have a feeling Autumn is within our reach," Lucy said. "About Linnea, I'm not so certain."

The maple trees on the street already showed their crimson color, a grim reminder that time was passing too rapidly as it invariably does in mid-August. In a few weeks, leaves would fly through the air, piling up on sidewalks and lawns. Fall had its own magic, but for the hundredth time, I decried the passing of summer with its gift of endless free days.

I'd have to solve the mystery before school started.

Linnea lived in a charming little cottage-type house painted soft pink with fresh aqua accents. It reminded me of an illustration in a children's picture book. A white picket fence enclosed the back yard. No dog rushed to the gate barking, although a whimsical sign cut in the shape of a rough collie warned a trespasser to 'Beware of the Dog.' The canine guardian was elsewhere, and in spite of its visual appeal, the place had an unmistakable look of abandonment.

Nonetheless, we walked up to the porch. On either side, two Alberta pines and a pair of spreading blue junipers cried out for water, their dry, yellowing branches hinting at approaching death. Beneath a bay window, a glorious bed of blue and pink hydrangeas flourished amid the weeds.

"She isn't here," Lucy said as I rang the doorbell. "Linnea took pride in her garden. She wouldn't neglect her yard if she were home."

Still, we waited for the sound of footsteps on the other side of the door.

Lucy lifted the top of the mailbox. "Empty."

"That tells me she planned to be gone," I said. "She probably placed a hold on her mail or asked a neighbor to collect it." I paused, considering. "How could she abandon her dog and leave her for others to find?"

"She may not have left willingly," Lucy pointed out.

"She was trying to travel back to the past," I said. "Whatever happened, where does that leave us?"

"Where we were before," Lucy said.

"Then we'll concentrate on finding Autumn," I said.

~ * ~

After dropping Lucy off at home, I took a detour to Clovers, knowing that Annica had an afternoon shift. She'd planned to sleep in after her big night.

A wave of cool air engulfed me as I opened the door. As usual, the dessert carousel drew my first attention. Every tart and cake and pie paid homage to Clover's Strawberry Week. Annica wore her strawberry earrings and a high-waisted pink maxi dress. I fell into an instant strawberry mood.

After I seated myself at my favorite booth, Annica joined me. She looked happy. "I have fifteen minutes free."

"I take it the evening went well," I said.

"Surprisingly, yes. Alethea was nice to me. She complimented my earrings and my dress."

"Alethea nice? Does a leopard change its spots?"

Marcy approached with menus and water. "Can I interest you in something strawberry, Jennet?" she asked.

I couldn't resist. "A tart and a pot of tea."

"Annica?"

"I'll have the same. Something's bothering me, though. I don't trust her. This niceness is pure fake. She has a plan. I'm sure of it."

That was the Alethea I knew.

"You may not have to encounter her again," I said. "How many gala parties does she host in a season?"

"Who knows? The problem is Alethea invited me to join the Hunt Club. She said Brent would expect it, and I'd have to go hunting with him, too. I couldn't do that."

No, she couldn't. Nor could I. We were defenders of the fox and other helpless creatures.

"What did Brent say?" I asked.

"I didn't tell him. He's oblivious. I don't have anything in common with those fox hunters," Annica said.

"You're engaged to one."

"Brent belongs to the Hunt Club, but he spends more time rescuing dogs."

That was true, although Brent had been an ardent fox hunter when we'd first met. A long time ago. Before Annica. He'd been the Huntsman. Since that time, his interest in the pseudo sport appeared to have waned. He was loyal to his friends, however. Hence the problem.

Marcy set our tarts down, and I paused to admire the fanciful meringue strawberry that topped each one.

"That invitation," Annica added. "She must know I wouldn't be interested. Why did she mention it?"

"To pretend to be accepting of you, I suppose. To agitate you."

"Well, I guess don't have any immediate worries. I don't think."

"Consider yourself forewarned," I said.

She smiled. "And forearmed."

"Now, about Linnea Wilmott. Let me tell you my theory."

When I'd finished, Annica asked, "Do you think Linnea wants to come home?"

"I'm assuming she does. It's where she belongs."

But should I assume? I wasn't taking into consideration her desire to change her past. Most likely what she wanted was to keep traveling until she landed in the right year.

A stray thought wandered into my mind. If Linnea were successful, would Autumn be a part of her new future? Had we set ourselves the task of finding a dog that didn't exist?

The mere contemplation of time travel and its implications left me floundering.

"I couldn't live in a primitive time," Annica said. "What if I got sick and needed antibiotics?"

"That's a definite downside."

"I don't want to leave my life," Annica said. "It's perfect now. In fact, I'm going to start shopping for a wedding dress."

"So soon?"

"Brent mentioned he'd like us to have a winter wedding."

"This winter?"

"Christmas is my favorite holiday," Annica said. "We're thinking of Christmas Eve or Christmas Day."

My mind filled with glittering images. Fragrant white roses, antique lace, a towering cake. Lacy snowflakes.

Yes, a winter wonderland wedding. I could hardly wait. As matron of honor, I'd need a dress, too.

"Let's hurry and solve this mystery," I said. "I'm eager to move on."

Nineteen

I decided to proceed as if Linnea weren't returning to her previous life. Sitting on the porch with the dogs ranged around me, I couldn't stop thinking about her. At first, they weren't happy thoughts. Linnea wasn't blithely making a decision that would change her future for the better. She was trapped in the wrong time, and each new attempt to travel to her chosen year failed. Her frustration quickly turned to panic.

An unspoken rule of time travel gleaned from reading numerous stories, but nonetheless legitimate: Don't mess with time. It'll always defeat you.

At length, I turned to an alternate scenario: Linnea was a wife and mother, married to the man she had defied time to be with. Writing was her hobby, not her profession. She'd never met Lucy nor asked for my help, and she didn't have a collie named Autumn.

Did her series books still exist, moldering on some antique shop shelf? Whenever I entered the time-and-consequences territory, my heart started spinning.

I brought my thoughts to an abrupt standstill, sat back against the cushions, and drank my lemonade. This August was on schedule to break a record for heat and humidity. Before long, we'd have to retire to the air-conditioned house.

Moments before I heard barking, my collie pack shifted into high alert. Ginger was running free on the lane followed by Molly and Jennifer. The girls collapsed on the porch steps, flushed, their green Dogfinders shirts wrinkled and damp. Ginger completed her greeting and, uninvited, lapped water from the dogs' pail.

"Do you have news about Autumn?" I asked.

"Sorry. No." Jennifer pushed back a strand of hair that had escaped her long ponytail. "We have twenty people and one dog looking for her."

"A dog?"

"He's Captain Larkin's retired search-and-rescue retriever."

"We came for Autumn's picture," Molly said.

Had I said I would give them a picture? I didn't think so. It was time I supplied the girls with more information. To a point.

"I'm afraid I don't have one," I admitted.

Molly seemed incredulous. "We have thousands of pictures of Ginger."

"Probably Autumn's owner does too, but she's missing. I hoped I'd hear from her by now. Unfortunately, it didn't happen."

"So, no picture?"

"I've never set eyes on Autumn," I admitted. "All I know is her color and age. After being on her own all this time, she must be in poor condition—scrawny, coat a mess."

Living heaven knows where. Eating…I didn't want to think about it. Definitely staying out of sight.

"I imagine she'll be fearful," I said.

"Don't worry. We won't chase her. We all have bags of treats."

"Would you girls like some lemonade?" I asked.

Molly glanced at Jennifer, who shook her head. "We're good," she said.

Jennifer tugged on Ginger's collar. "Did you say Autumn ran away?"

"Yes, when she was spooked by thunder."

Molly leaned forward to pet Misty, who was shamelessly begging for attention. "Ginger doesn't like thunder either, but she stays in the house and sits quietly like a stone statue until the storm is over."

"At the time, Autumn was in a parked car. Her owner was there, but Autumn dashed past her."

"You said this happened near here?" Molly asked.

Near Huron Court, the most dangerous stretch of road in the county. I didn't say that.

"Not far from Sagramore Lake."

"There's lots of woods around here for a dog to hide in," Jennifer said, "and plenty of lakes so she won't be thirsty."

"With twenty people helping me look for her, there's hope," I said.

Jennifer stood and soothed her wrinkled shirt. "Let's go. We've been asking at all the houses on Sagramore Lake Road. Now we're going to branch out."

"Wish us luck," Molly added.

"Of course."

And they were off.

The dogs settled down. The lane was empty again. A slight breeze stole into the air and set the flowers a flutter. I finished my lemonade and considered a problem I'd done my best to sideline.

How could I search for Autumn in the one place she would almost certainly be without inviting disaster into my life?

~ * ~

After about a quarter of a mile, Huron Court turned into two separate roads.

Two roads diverged in a yellow wood...

It wasn't yellow, not yet, but a discernible band of gold wove its way through the leaves. For some reason, I had always taken the eastern half. That was where I'd met Violet Randall playing with her collie in front of the pink Victorian. Where Brent's magical wildflower field flourished in full sunlight. Where, without warning, the season could change from summer to winter as an unholy snow began to fall.

Today, I took Misty, Star, and Sky down the western half of the road. They were delighted at the extravagance of new scents, insisting on investigating each one.

I wondered if my choice in route would make all the difference. That was only a line in Frost's poem, but the parallel road was worth exploring. I had a feeling it was safe, that whatever malevolent power waited to whisk travelers off to another time stayed on the eastern side.

Don't trust every feeling. I could hear Lucy's warning carried on the breeze.

All right. I wouldn't, but so far nothing untoward had happened. If I had the slightest inkling of danger, I would retreat immediately.

On the verge, trees grew close together, their leaves forming a canopy that cast a shade on the road, but occasional patches of wildflowers painted vivid color on the landscape. It was a pretty walk, enlivened by birdsong. There wasn't a house in sight.

Frequent signs warned 'No Trespassing!' and 'Trespassers Will Be Prosecuted.' The road curved, then I caught a glimpse of blue shining through the woods. A lake. And just ahead...Could that be a path?

Yes. I went closer. But a narrow one, scarcely wide enough for two to walk abreast. A large branch lay across the entrance, its leaves withered and shaking in the breeze.

I studied the unexpected opening, although I didn't intend to turn off the main half-road. Leave it to the young and fit and the search-and-rescue dog.

Oh, for goodness sake, Jennet, when did you become a coward? What happened to 'leave no stone unturned?' Don't all paths lead somewhere?

"All right," I said. "Just a little way. No more than a dozen steps."

At my encouragement, all three collies jumped over the barrier. My little agility stars. Emboldened, Misty yanked on the leash. I tightened my hold.

Stepping over the branch, I stood on a jumble of rocks scattered in deadwood and leaves left over from past autumns. I couldn't see far as the path twisted its way out of sight. Depending on its length, it would empty out on the eastern half of Huron Court. Or perhaps it would end before reaching that point.

Left to her own devices, Misty would have plunged ahead, taking me with her, but I resisted, keeping my eyes peeled on the unstable ground.

At her sudden high screech, I looked up. An animal form leaped out of the woods, soared high above the trail, and melted into the mist that came creeping out from the other side.

Mist?

Where had the mist come from on a warm, sunny afternoon?

I had no idea, but all of a sudden it was there. Like a living thing, it slithered toward me, gauze-like arms reaching out to handy trunks, spiraling around them. Coming closer.

Move!

"Run!" I turned the dogs around and headed back the way we'd come away from Huron Court. East or west, it was still the same road.

Twenty

Was the mist following me?

I looked back. It seemed to have stopped before reaching the road. Still a trace of it hung in the air, thick and moist. I could almost taste it.

I had encountered mist before, on the other half of Huron Court. It often heralded the appearance of a wandering spirit. Or a shift in time. Nothing I wanted to experience.

Keep walking.

A more important question. That animal I'd seen so briefly. Was it a deer? Or a dog? Could it have been Autumn?

I tried to call back the image, but my mind refused to cooperate. An animal the color of autumn leaves. Moving more swiftly than thought.

Can't you tell a deer from a dog?

Usually, but the creature had come and gone too quickly, before my awareness caught up to my vision. It could as easily have been an illusion, the mist forming an animal shape the way a cloud often does.

At any rate, I wasn't going back to investigate. I had no doubt the mist still moved listlessly through the woods. Was it contained on Huron Court or could it someday steal over the beach and advance on Jonquil Lane?

A nightmare thought best pushed to the back of my consciousness at least until I was safe home.

I left Huron Court and walked along the lake and on to Jonquil Lane, all without incident. Away from the water, the sun seemed to grow hotter with every step. The dogs lagged behind, showing less interest in enticing scents and growing excited at the sight of our house. I, too, could hardly wait to cool off and unwind at home.

When I unlocked the door, they nearly dragged me inside. We headed for the kitchen where we all drank our fill of fresh, cold water.

Well, that was quite an experience. I had allowed myself to be chased away from my walk by condensation. From another perspective, it was known as self-preservation.

To banish morbid fantasies, I straightened the house and made a stew. The dogs, the lucky ones, rested. While our dinner cooked, I baked a chocolate cake.

A glance at the calendar told me that my free days were numbered. For all the angst that went hand-and-glove with teaching, the environment at Marston was wholesome. No time tangles to unravel. No living mists to wrap around the school. No elusive collie to roam forever beyond my reach.

I wondered if we would ever find Autumn.

~ * ~

At times, I thought Brent's sixth sense told him when I was making something especially good for dinner, for invariably on those days he showed up with treats for the collies and flowers or candy for me.

I wasn't surprised, therefore, when the dogs alerted me to company and I saw Brent's vintage Plymouth turn into our driveway. The sunlight gave the car's green fins an emerald shine.

He took a shopping bag out of the back seat and made his way up the walkway, waving to the collies who had gathered at the bay window. Being familiar with Pluto's Gourmet Pet Shop bags and the wonders they contained, they rushed the door before it was properly opened.

"I smell stew," Brent announced as he handed me the dog treats and distributed pats to his fan base.

"I hope you can stay for dinner," I said. "I have chocolate cake, too."

"Don't mind if I do."

He followed me to the kitchen where I'd been halted in the middle of making a salad. I expected Crane any minute, but I was eager to share my afternoon adventure with someone. I brought two cans of ginger ale out of the refrigerator and sat with him at the oak table, telling him of the illusory animal born of the mist.

"You were smart to high tail it out of there," he said. "We don't want another lady lost in time." He pried the can open. "That writer is still missing, I take it?"

"She's not at her house and hasn't been in touch with us. So, I guess, yes."

As I hadn't seen Brent for a while, he didn't know my theory that Linnea had been stranded in the early nineteenth century where she'd written at least one book. Unless Annica had told him, but no. He was surprised, almost incredulous at the idea that she had stayed in the past that long.

"It sounds farfetched. But who knows?" He took a swig of his drink. "It's funny. People tend to disappear around you, Jennet. Like that woman whose dog vanished at the walkathon."

"Ellalyn," I said. "You're right. I'm a jinx. But this is the first person who's disappeared in time."

I marveled at how naturally we talked about time travel as if it were an everyday occurrence. Only in Foxglove Corners.

"I've got a weird story of my own," Brent said. "I hired a new guy, Doug. He gives the collies who stay at the barn their evening meal. A couple of days ago, he fed one I don't even have."

"I don't understand."

"He didn't have enough dinners fixed, so he had to go get another one. It looks like I have an extra collie."

"And we have a missing collie. Did Doug say if one of the dogs was a sable?"

Brent laughed. "He doesn't know that term. Doug just said I had a bonus Lassie."

"Is he right? Is there an extra collie hanging out at the barn?"

"Not when I'm there," he said. "So I figure it's a stray. The food's good at our place," he added.

"And it only turns up at feeding time. Clever pooch. I'll bet it's Autumn. She's the only missing collie in Foxglove Corners. That I know of."

"Now I'm curious," he said. "I'll feed the dogs their dinner tonight. If an extra one pops up, how will I know if it's Autumn?"

"Say her name. She won't be well groomed like your collies."

"I'll let you know," he said. "In the meantime, I'll swing by Huron Court. I'd like to see that mist on the trail, and maybe that's where the beggar collie hangs out."

"Don't disappear."

"I don't plan to," he said.

Twenty-one

After an unsuccessful search for the perfect wedding dress at the Maplewood Mall, Annica and I decided to visit a recently opened vintage bridal shop on Antique Row in Lakeville.

"If I don't find a dress I like there, they may have some interesting accessories," Annica said.

"Like earrings?"

"I'm going to wear the emeralds Brent gave me. But I can always use more earrings."

She must have hundreds of pairs already, ranging from elaborate teardrop styles to the kind that complemented Clovers' desserts like her trusty strawberries and pumpkins.

"I want a dress that's different," she said. "Something wonderful."

If we came home empty-handed, at least we would have a girls' day out. September was rapidly approaching, which meant school for me and two new English courses for Annica, along with her job at Clovers. Suddenly it seemed that winter was pushing at the gates, bypassing fall. Had we started shopping in time?

Yesteryear's Brides was a small store with a single dress in the window, a fairy tale concoction of embroidery and lace worn by a mannequin with long blond hair. A veil sprinkled with glitter pooled gracefully around her silver-slippered feet.

Annica frowned. "It's way too fussy. Not me."

I agreed. "Let's see what else they have."

We entered to the chiming of bells and found ourselves in a world of white. A spicy fragrance scented the air, perhaps emanating from the bouquet of snowy flowers on a round table. Or were they silk? I touched a rose petal. No, they were real, but their combined perfume, while initially pleasing, was too potent for my taste.

At first, I thought the store appeared to be unattended, then a small lady in a navy blue skirt and ruffled white blouse appeared from behind a display of veils on a row of disembodied heads.

She looked from me to Annica and let her gaze rest on Annica. "Good afternoon, ladies. Which one of you is the bride-to-be?"

"I am, but we're just browsing," Annica said. "Trying to get an idea. I'm not sure I want an old-time dress."

"That's our specialty," the lady said crisply. From her expression, she might have added, "Why did you come to a vintage store then?"

"We're looking," Annica said. "Are these dresses truly vintage or imitations?"

"They're absolutely one hundred percent authentic." She pointed to a dress with puffy sleeves worn by another blond mannequin. "This is the gown made especially for the one and only Amanda Winchester."

I had never heard of her.

Annica nodded. "It's lovely, but I'd like something a little less fancy."

"A wedding dress should be fancy," the salesperson said.

"Not necessarily."

"The fancier the better. It's a woman's one day to shine."

I thought a bride could very well shine in a plain white dress with classic lines. Especially a beauty like Annica with her bright red-gold hair.

"Miss Venn's vintage collection is the best in the state of Michigan, bar none," the saleslady said. "Every dress is a masterpiece. It's unique."

"Miss Venn?" I said.

"Miss Alethea Venn. She chose each gown personally. Miss Venn has impeccable taste."

Annica glanced at me. I knew what she was thinking.

"I don't know," she said. "I think we're going to have to leave. I feel ill," she added. "All of a sudden."

"Well, really...Don't rush off. I may have just the dress for you in back..."

"Thanks anyway." I took Annica's arm. "Let's get you some fresh air," I said.

Outside I took a deep breath, glad to leave the oppressive scent and the officious saleslady behind.

"Alethea," Annica murmured. "Who knew she was anything but a fox hunter?"

"Not I," I said. "How did you hear about Yesteryear's Brides?"

"From a customer. She admired my ring and asked when I was getting married. She said I should check out Yesterday's Brides. I'd never ever buy a dress from Alethea Venn's shop."

"No," I said. "There are plenty of other bridal stores."

"It would be bad luck," she said.

"I wouldn't go that far."

"I feel like I've tempted fate even to stop there. There's something creepy about that place. Those heads. Yikes."

"Well, we didn't know it was Alethea's shop, and we didn't stay long."

But how odd to discover that Alethea owned a bridal shop just when Annica and Brent were planning their wedding. It must be a coincidence. How could it be anything else?

"I'm out of the mood to look for a wedding dress," she said. "The Green House is having a summer sale. Maybe we can find some bargains."

~ * ~

The dull orange book on the side table served as a pedestal for a crystal candlestick. No doubt customers were intended to notice the candlestick, which was quite lovely, but I was no ordinary customer.

This lone volume didn't have a dust jacket. A purple stain marred the upper right corner, and a quarter-sized piece was missing from the cover.

I couldn't pass it by without reading the title.

Could it be? Yes. By some miracle, in my hand I held the book, *Linda Welcsh in the Wild West*, the one the Green House supposedly didn't have.

I opened it, noting yellow paper rough to the touch. minute tears, and scribbles in the margin. But it was intact, readable, and would possibly help me in my dual searches. Was my luck finally turning?

Twenty-two

As soon as I tended to the dogs and dinner, I made myself comfortable in the rocker and opened my book, hoping to find additional proof that Linnea Wilmott had written the series and perhaps left a clue to her whereabouts.

Hope springs eternal.

Linda's great-great-great grandfather had been a sheriff in the Colorado Territory. She had long admired a daguerreotype of him in an old photograph album. Now that she had access to a time machine, she thought it would be a lark to visit his town with her traveling companions and perhaps meet him.

Because this was an adventure story, the girls' day trip in time turned into an unlikely romp with cowboys, outlaws, and Indians. They met the sheriff, who was every bit as handsome and charismatic as Linda had imagined, but, of course, she didn't reveal their relationship.

Two hundred pages later, they were safe back in Professor Welsch's laboratory, although Annie was feeling feverish and wondered if she'd brought a nineteenth century disease back to the present.

We didn't find out. The last paragraph was a preview of the third book in the series, *Linda Welsch in the Time of the Dinosaurs*. I read the preview: A malfunction in the time machine sends the girls into the distant past where they dodge a nasty tempered T-rex and hostile cavemen.

Together in one age?

Here was another book to look for, although so far reading the series hadn't been helpful.

Except it made me wonder. What if I could control when I went and for how long, the way Linda Welsch did? What an adventure that would be!

Where, with all of history available to me, would I go? A relatively safe destination, a time with no wars and no pandemics. A year of peace and prosperity. Past or future?

Smiling at my own fancies, I went into the kitchen to check on my roast.

Home, I thought. Home is best.

~ * ~

The next morning, I received a text message from Jennifer: 'Autumn sighting more later.'

How infuriating not to have details. Where was Autumn when they saw her? Were they able to lure her with treats? And when would Jennifer send another text?

At present all I could do was wait. Why not make the most of a lull in the craziness and do nothing? Before long, I would be in my classroom wearing one of my new fall dresses and opening my American literature textbook to Puritan writings. Getting to know my students and having a rushed lunch in the school courtyard with Leonora. Keeping out of the way of Principal Grimsley. The time travels of Linnea Willmott would be a distant memory. Autumn would be found.

What I did on my summer vacation...

The dogs followed me to the porch where I sank into the rocker and surveyed my surroundings. My home. Across the lane, the yellow Victorian. Camille's amazing flowers splashed the landscape with vivid color for all that summer was winding down. In my own flowerbeds, the weeds were thriving. Let them. It was late August, after all.

I was on the verge of dozing when a faint ting alerted me to another text. This one, from Jennifer, was even shorter than the first. 'Got her coming home.'

Wonderful. One problem solved. All was (almost) right with the world.

~ * ~

A few hours later, the sun disappeared and rain clouds floated low in a sullen sky. The humid air was potent enough to steal breath. Misty whimpered and nudged my knee. She lay at my feet, her eyes on the lane where nothing stirred, at least nothing visible to human eyes.

A frightening foreboding stole into my thoughts.

Something bad is going to happen.

It may have already happened.

Nothing will ever be the same.

Always remember this brief time of peace and contentment. It may never come again.

By evening, I understood. The premonition had heralded a grim reality. Jennifer and Molly were missing, along with Ginger.

Once a week, the girls called a short, informal meeting of Dogfinders, Inc. The members compared notes, shared information and pictures, and made plans. The meetings were usually held in Molly's house, and they took pride in providing refreshments as they had once stocked their lemonade stand.

Today they missed their own meeting. It grew late, and they didn't come home. Nor did Ginger. In a panic, their parents notified the police and before long an Amber alert flashed on my phone screen.

They had been out looking for a lost dog.

Autumn.

But they had found her. They were on their way home. I relayed my information to the police and waited all evening for another text message. It wasn't forthcoming.

Where could two girls and two collies go?

I was afraid I knew the answer: Into the mist.

Twenty-three

After I had time to examine this latest disappearance from all angles, I doubted that Molly and Jennifer and the two collies had been swept into another time. It was perhaps wistful thinking, but it seemed that to date, to my knowledge, time travel had been a solitary experience. Annica, Brent, and I had lost our hold on the present separately as had Linnea. Was a party of four—two young girls, two dogs—somehow protected by size alone?

Were there any rules?

If they hadn't vanished into another time, where were they?

I should have warned them to stay away from Huron Court. Why hadn't I? Knowledge was power, and guilt is a hard burden to cast off.

"It wasn't your fault, Jennet," Crane assured me the next morning. "How could it be? Molly and Jennifer and their friends have searched all over the county for missing dogs. Anything could have happened to them. They should have taken another person along with them, somebody older."

Would it have made a difference?

"Jennifer said they'd found Autumn," I reminded him. "They were coming home. Then something happened."

I broke my toast into little pieces. It didn't taste good. And I hadn't touched the scrambled eggs. Wherever Jennifer and Molly and the dogs were, did they have anything to eat?

I remembered they had been missing before, taken to a remote location and abandoned by a boy playing a stupid trick on them. That had turned out all right. I remembered, too, that one of the Dogfinders, a captain of something or other, had a search-and-rescue dog. And I remembered Brent's half-teasing remark that people around me tended to disappear.

I'd have to let Brent know what had happened. He would set aside his day's agenda to join in the search.

"The girls have each other and two dogs with them," Crane reminded me.

"Heroic collies," I added.

An encouraging thought to begin the day.

If ever there were a time when I needed Lucy's input, this was it. As soon as Crane left for his patrol, I drove to Dark Gables. I wasn't surprised that Lucy knew about the girls' disappearance. I was heartened that she'd had one of her premotions concerning them.

"They're all right," Lucy said, "all four of them. They're in another place, but they'll be home soon."

"You should let their parents know."

"I will, but they may not believe me."

"They don't know your reputation."

"That sounds ominous."

"Where is this place?" I asked.

"That I don't know. I see them on a desolate beach in winter. The lake water is hard as glass with isles of snow floating on it. They're somewhere in the past or future."

I had finished my tea, which tasted better than the coffee I'd tried to drink at breakfast. "I want to know if I'm going to be involved."

"Surely you're not planning to. The police are equipped to do their jobs."

"The police don't know the secret of Huron Court."

"Nor do most people."

I prepared my cup for reading and sat back in the wicker sofa to listen to Lucy's predictions.

She was quiet for a while, thoughtful, turning the cup to the jangle of the gold Zodiac charms on her bracelet. "The formations are in a muddle today," she said. "They reflect your mental state."

"Can you see anything all?"

"Your wish is here."

"That's good."

"And a danger sign. It's large and practically flashing in the cup. Right in your home." She pointed to a tea leaf that looked ordinary to me.

"This is possible danger for you," she added.

"Not so good."

"Only if you plow through. When does school start?"

"For students, next Monday. Teachers have to report on Thursday."

"You won't have much time to get in trouble then."

I nodded. "The first weeks are especially busy. Then there's the long commute. Jennifer and Molly were looking forward to their new classes," I added. "They're good students. Good at everything they do."

"Don't worry. They'll come home. I'm certain of it, and Autumn will be with them."

"Everyone except Linnea."

"Linnea." Lucy's gaze came to rest on the dark woods at the back of her property. "Linnea's fate may remain a mystery. We have to remind ourselves that she wanted to travel back in time."

"Yes, to a specific year to make a different life decision."

"You can't bend time to your will," Lucy said. "We tried to warn her."

Lucy sounded as if she had given up on Linnea. I still hoped for a happy ending for her. Perhaps I'd have to be satisfied with the return of Autumn."

If that were going to happen.

~ * ~

At home I called Brent on his cell phone and waited to hear his familiar voice boom out a hearty greeting.

What I heard was a record inviting me to leave a message.

Well, he had many interests, along with a new fiancée. He couldn't forever be at my beck and call. I was, however, vaguely apprehensive.

"People around you tend to disappear," he had said.

Telling myself that Brent would return my call later, I turned my energy to dinner, cooking a roast so I would have plenty to serve if Brent showed up.

By now, he should have called me back. If he were going to.

My apprehension turned to genuine worry.

People around me tended to vanish. Case in point: Molly and Jennifer, two girls I cared deeply about.

Jennet, you are indeed a jinx.

I waited three hours and called Brent again. Listened to his recorded voice again. Left another message.

The clock struck four. Crane would be home soon. I could hardly wait. Everything was better when he was with me.

Twenty-four

"I'm worried about Brent," Annica said the next morning.

She set a doughnut and a cup of hot chocolate in front of me and joined me in my favorite booth. Clovers was uncharacteristically quiet with few customers. The mood bordered on somber.

I was worried as well, but waited to hear her reason before speaking.

"Why?"

"He stood me up last night. We had a date, just for coffee, but he didn't show up and he didn't call. That's not like him."

"I tried to reach him, too."

As she touched her engagement ring, her voice trembled. "It's Alethea Venn. She's luring him away from me."

I was half-afraid to speculate on Brent's unaccustomed silence, but never in a million years had I thought Alethea was responsible for it.

"That isn't going to happen, Annica."

"She's determined and evil. Her being nice to me was just a ruse to throw me off balance. I talked to Doug at the barn," she added. "Brent wasn't there. That's unusual but not unheard of. What do you think? Have I lost my fiancé?"

"Hardly. You just misplaced him."

The last time I had seen Brent, I'd told him about going to the fork in Huron Court and taking the other road. He'd been intrigued by the trail and the mist and planned to investigate.

If he had done so...

When I told Annica about our conversation, she brightened. "That's where he went then. Maybe he stumbled over a branch and hit his head on a rock and lost consciousness."

"Talk about a worst-case scenario. He wouldn't stay unconscious. Brent is strong and resourceful."

"Jennet, we have to help him. Should I call the police?"

"Don't jump to conclusions. It's too early to report him missing."

"This trail in the woods...We can check it out ourselves."

I thought of a danger sign flashing in my teacup. Just a bit of Red Rose. Or was it a true warning? I had entered the trail with Misty on a previous occasion and nothing earthshaking had happened.

Nothing? I'd quickly retreated after seeing something. An animal?

Run again at the first sign of trouble, I told myself. There's safety in numbers.

"If we're very, very careful," I said.

"We will be, of course. When can we go?"

"When are you free?"

"In fifteen minutes," she said. "I'm working a split shift today."

"All right then." I swirled the mini-marshmallows through the chocolate mixture and caught one on the spoon.

That would give me time to eat my doughnut.

~ * ~

A light morning mist lingered over the road. Perfectly natural. No cause for alarm. So I told myself. Not every mist is born of ominous origins.

I drove slowly, looking for the trail, for a large fallen branch blocking the entrance. I saw nothing but thick woodland and bright wildflowers.

"I don't see anything that looks like a trail," Annica said.

"It's a little further."

"I'd rather it was Alethea than an accident," she said after a moment.

"It's probably neither."

"Why didn't he answer my call then?"

"I don't know. You'll have a chance to ask him."

"Promise?"

I didn't answer.

"There it is." I brought the car to a stop and parked as close to the verge as possible. Chances were no other car would come along.

"Let's walk a way," I said. "Not too far, or we may find ourselves coming out on the other road."

Annica was the first to step over the branch, showing every indication of pushing her way through the encroaching vegetation.

"Slow down," I said. "You'll get your foot caught in a vine and fall."

She grabbed for a seedling, not as stable as it looked, and surveyed the trail spread out in front of us. It looked narrower today as if, since I'd last seen it, the wilderness had advanced several inches.

What, I wondered, or who, had made the path?

"He came this way," she said. "I can feel it."

The mist appeared suddenly without warning. Wispy streamers swirling through green growth. They looked like strands of earthborn clouds.

I reached for Annica's arm. "We have to go back."

"Why?"

"Don't you see it?"

"That little bit of mist? It won't hurt us. We can't leave Brent."

"We don't know he's here."

"But if he is..."

I had a feeling, too. If Brent had once been here, he wasn't anymore.

With every second, the mist appeared to draw closer. As it had before. It was no longer isolated wisps. It was bearing down on us.

"Now, Annica!" I cried.

"Well, okay, but I'm calling the police."

"Do what you think best, but do it from a distance."

How far to the car? How far had we walked?

We backtracked, moving faster than was prudent, considering the treacherous ground. Annica raced ahead, although she had been loath to cut our search short.

For no apparent reason, my heart began to pound. The humidity had caught up to me, dampening my blouse. My neck felt wet. I swiped at it impatiently, wishing for a tissue.

A sudden wrench yanked me to my knees. A vine hidden under a layer of leaves had latched onto my ankle, wrapping itself around my foot as if it were alive. I tugged at the thick, tough stem; it seemed to tug back.

"Annica!" I cried. "Can you help me?"

She didn't answer. I couldn't see her, dear Lord, couldn't see the trail now. It seemed to have shrunk to a ribbon. Wet leaves slapped my bare arms. The mist had overtaken me.

Between one step and the next? How was that possible?

You shouldn't be able to touch mist, but this mist made its own rules. It was cold. Solidifying. Tenacious. I felt as if I were encased in a block of rapidly forming ice.

I stood and tried to free my foot, but the vine held me in a death grip.

In my purse, which I'd left in the car, I had a pair of manicure scissors. They weren't ideal to free myself from a thick vine but were better than nothing. No point in thinking about them, though, as they might as well be at home.

As suddenly as it had appeared, the mist dissipated, leaving behind a blurry wet landscape. I found myself surrounded by green. Trees and plants pressed close to me. The ribbon trail had vanished.

Where was I?

I called Annica again, and my voice bounced back to me. Surely she was close enough to hear me. But everything had changed. I sensed that I was alone in an alien, hostile wood, still held fast by a wretched vine.

Did this mean I had traveled in time?

What now?

Twenty-five

Find the road. So what if the trail is gone? Squeeze through the trees and underbrush. Get to the car. But first, break the vine's hold.

I had a sick feeling I wouldn't find Annica.

Reality check. I had traveled in time, either to the past before the trail had been cut, or to the future when the woods had long since reclaimed their own. And whichever way I'd gone, my car wouldn't have accompanied me.

Desperation gave me the strength to free myself from the vine, leaving me with a nasty red circle on my ankle. When I'd gotten dressed this morning, I hadn't expected to go tramping through a wilderness.

Suddenly, I thought of Linnea, thrust into a winter storm dressed in jeans and a sleeveless top. When time casts you out of your rightful place in the universe, you don't have a chance to dress for the event or pack necessities. All I had was...Nothing. Not even a path to walk on.

Correction. I had the keys in my pocket. But not the car.

Fortunately, the season hadn't changed. If anything, it was hotter than it had been before.

I fought back the panic and tried to think clearly. If I'd moved in time, that didn't mean I'd also been flung from my space. We hadn't walked far when I'd seen the first wisps of mist, perhaps a quarter of a mile or less. I'd simply retrace my steps, and, assuming I'd chosen the right direction, would soon emerge on the road.

It wasn't as if I'd been dropped down into the heart of the wood. It only felt like that. Shimmering leaves coated with moisture slapped against my legs and arms, and my legs began to itch.

This was sheer misery.

Breathe!

I couldn't fill my lungs with air.

Don't think about it. Just do it.

All right. That worked. I started to walk, pushing encroaching plant life out of my way, my eyes fixed on the ground, lest I step into another rapacious vine. Again, I was aware of my pounding heart. I felt the painful sting of a thorn on my hand as I touched a thistle-like stalk, and the itching in my legs had gone from annoying to intolerable.

The estimated quarter of a mile or less seemed to go on forever. I never aspired to be a trailblazer, but Fate hadn't given me a choice. I had to keep moving or be lost forever.

Maybe I was lost, no matter what I did.

Gradually, the woods thinned, and the next plodding steps brought me to a narrow verge overgrown with yellow wildflowers that resembled lilies. I didn't recall seeing them before, and there was no fallen branch. Was this the place at which we'd entered the trail? It was hard to tell if I was in a different time.

I didn't see my car. Well, I hadn't expected to. Still, the presence of the keys in my pocket was a source of slight comfort.

Annica, where are you?

While I had traveled in time, she'd remained behind. I had thought there would be safety in numbers. Well, I'd been wrong before. I had to deal with the situation that now faced me.

I walked on, knowing I couldn't hope to encounter a passing motorist as Huron Court, east and west, was a lightly traveled road. With no other option, I kept going, heading in the direction of Jonquil Lane.

Or so I hoped.

~ * ~

The season was the same, late summer with subtle signs of fall. It was still hot and humid, and I longed for a shower and dry clothes, but that had become an impossible dream. With every step, I wondered what I would find when I reached my home.

Subconsciously, I waited to hear Brent's booming voice as he came up behind me. Had he ended up in the same time, only in another place? And were Molly and Jennifer here, too, with the dogs?

Unlikely, but the company of my friends would turn this nightmare into an adventure.

At length, I rounded a curve and came to a large blue-sided house set far back from the road. It was one of those popular structures referred to as McMansions, and I noted with dismay that the landscaping appeared to have been in place for a long time.

When was the house built? And was it one of many?

That probably meant I was in the future because nothing had been built on Huron Court since the burning of Violet Randall's pink Victorian. I was momentarily heartened at the thought of company in this lonely world, not to mention the opportunity of learning to what year I had been transported, but I hesitated.

Imagine the homeowner's reaction to the appearance of a stranger with ripped, grass-stained clothing saying, "Would you please tell me what year it is?"

I didn't have a chance to find out as no one was home.

Now, should I rest on the porch and be mistaken for a vagrant or keep walking?

My answer came in the form of a distant sound of thunder.

Keep walking, I decided.

Into the storm.

Twenty-six

The storm consisted of faraway rumbling and a scattering of warm raindrops that did no harm. Then it was over. I was lucky. Well, relatively lucky. I was still lost in an alien time but wasn't drenched and in danger of catching a cold.

By the time I reached the fork in the road, I had passed two more McMansions. One had a 'For Sale' sign in the front yard; the other looked deserted. Perhaps they were infrequently visited vacation houses. Did the homeowners know their mansions occupied the most dangerous road in Foxglove Corners, the one with a fragile hold on time? No matter, the scent of lake water in the air told me I was almost home.

In due time I reached the lake, that familiar body of water on whose beach I'd walked the dogs and often met Molly and Jennifer with Ginger. Today, lake and beach were deserted, still water shimmering in the heat of early morning.

Was it September in this time, I wondered, and were the young people in school? That was an easy answer, but not the correct one, I suspected.

Back in my own time, had the girls been found in time to go back to school? And had Brent made his way home? Which reminded me of

Annica. Why had I been the one to slip out of time when we had been walking so close to each other while exiting the woods?

You stepped on an enchanted inch of ground, I told myself. Annica stepped around it.

A burst of energy enabled me to walk briskly down Sagramore Lake Road and from there to Jonquil Lane which looked—thank you, God—the same as it had when I had set out for Clovers this morning. Or an unspecified number of years ago. Any minute now, I would hear the dogs barking their welcome, see their faces squished together in the front window.

One more curve.

It didn't happen.

My house looked the same with its soft green color and gingerbread trim, and the stained glass between the double turrets held the rays of sunlight as usual. But something was different.

The silence.

No dogs barking. No birds singing. No rustling in the woods across the lane.

My car was gone, of course, as was Crane's Jeep. He was on duty. The yellow Victorian had the desolate appearance of a house left to its own devices. Perhaps Camille and Gilbert had taken the dogs to Tennessee for their annual fall vacation.

My heart rate, which had returned to its normal pattern, began to race again. There must be a logical explanation for the emptiness and unnatural stillness that hung over the lane.

Where were the dogs? Where were the people?

Faded purple coneflowers beaten down by rain provided the only color in a landscape that seemed suddenly drab and bleak, and a black wreath hung on the door. Black?

I stood still, staring at it. I'd never seen it before and would never have bought it, preferring colorful silk flowers and bright trailing ribbons.

Every instinct told me to freeze in my tracks. Because once I entered my home—this house—I would possess knowledge that I didn't want.

One can't hide from reality, however, and I'd reached my destination.

I slid the key in the lock. At this point, I would be surprised if it didn't work, but the door swung open, and I stepped inside into thick and all-pervading silence.

Crane would be patrolling the roads and by-roads of Foxglove Corners, I assumed, oblivious of my dilemma. Still, I called his name, and my heart sank as an echo answered me.

Where were my eight collies?

Calling anyone was useless. I was obviously alone, not only in my own home. Possibly in the world. I was lost in time, wandering in a Ray Bradbury world.

I sank into my rocker, which was miraculously still there. And there were my time travel books, neatly stacked on the coffee table with my favorite mug on top of them, the one decorated with the image of a collie puppy.

A horrifying thought surfaced. I had died back there on Huron Court when I'd fallen. I was a spirit, one of the ghosts that haunted the most beautiful part of Foxglove Corners.

It must be. Why else would a black wreath hang on the door?

This, however, didn't answer the crucial question: Where was everybody?

~ * ~

Eventually I rose and set out on an exploratory trip of my own home. The kitchen was in pristine condition but different. The Lassie tin where I kept the dogs' treats held only a few crumbs. The refrigerator was almost empty with food I didn't remember buying. There was no meat defrosting, no milk or juice, no cake in the tin on the counter; and the teapot on the stove was dusty. The dogs' food dishes and water bowls were stored under the sink.

Empty. Everything empty. Empty was the watchword.

Upstairs. The bed was neatly made, as I'd left it this morning—or whatever morning I'd last been in the house. I opened the closet. My clothes were there. I'd forgotten the sad state of my denim skirt and white shirt. Mechanically. I pulled out a navy blue skirt and white blouse and tossed them on the bed.

The bathroom. The water was running, nice and hot, and clean towels hung on the rack. The way I'd left them.

Dead or alive, I could take a shower and wash my hair, apply fresh makeup. The idea made me smile—almost.

Did I need to do that being a ghost?

Stop! I ordered myself.

I didn't die. I said it aloud, the words echoing in the lonely hallway. Something weird was going on, something else, and if I waited, everything that was wrong would right itself. Crane would come home at his usual time. He'd taken the dogs to the groomer or the vet.

All eight of them?

They'd tangled with a skunk. It was possible.

I could call Annica and ask her what had happened...

...on that day.

It'll be all right.

I peeled off my clothes, stepped into the shower and adjusted the water.

It'll be all right all right all right...

As soon as Crane came home. As soon as I learned where my dogs were. As soon as I talked to Annica. As soon as I...

I'd go through the house again, check all the rooms, find something to eat. There must be something I could eat in my own refrigerator.

Why was the Lassie tin empty? I had eight collies.

Had? Not had, have. I just didn't know where they were.

Downstairs the clock chimed twice.

Now all I needed to know was the year.

Twenty-seven

I left the house and gazed longingly at the yellow Victorian, thinking that sharing tea and muffins in Camille's country kitchen could shrink the greatest of problems to manageable size.

Wishful thinking. Camille wasn't there and had taken her kindness and caring with her.

You're on your own, Jennet. Without transportation, without your loved ones, without an anchor.

It occurred to me that I could go back inside and wait to see if Crane would come home at his usual time. Then I glanced again at the black wreath on the door.

He thought I was dead. He had taken the dogs away. The green Victorian farmhouse was no longer his home.

Where was he? And why was it so quiet? Where had all the birds gone?

Most important, where was I? Not in the world I knew.

Unbidden, a poignant scene from *Our Town* formed in my mind. Emily returns from the dead to witness a scene from her life. It proves to be too much for her to bear, and she returns happily to her grave.

The similarities weren't strong, but memories of playing with my collies were so painful, I felt a sharp jab in my chest. I could almost hear Halley and Candy play-growling over possession of the Frisbee and see Misty wandering as close to the edge of the lane as she dared and Crane...

"I'm not dead." I said this aloud. "I'm here." And I was wallowing in indecision.

In the end, I could think of only one course of action. I could walk back to Huron Court and hope, pray, that time would return me to my proper year—to a few seconds before I took that final, fatal step.

This time, if I were granted the opportunity, I would follow Annica, stay close to her, and watch for that small section of ground where the vine had entrapped me. And hope Time would reverse its action and let a different scenario unfold.

My car would be parked on the verge where I'd left it. I'd drive away, drop Annica off at her home, and go on with my day. Brent and the girls would still be missing, but Crane would come home at the end of his shift.

Home?

Yes. The green Victorian farmhouse on Jonquil Lane would be my home again. All that would happen, but first, I yanked the black wreath off the door and tossed it into the closest flower bed.

I wasn't dead!

The unnerving silence broke apart as high-pitched barking erupted in the woods across the lane. In the next instant, Misty bounded out of the darkness and barreled into me. I fell backward into a patch of coneflowers, and she licked my face, all the while whimpering like an abandoned baby. It was the most piteous sound I'd ever heard. And the most welcome.

My beautiful Misty girl. I pulled her close, hugged her, and kissed the top of her soft head.

I wasn't alone. No woman who has the love of a dog is ever alone, no matter how bizarre the circumstances.

Unfortunately, dogs can't talk. Nonetheless, I bombarded Misty with questions.

"Where are they, Misty? What happened to the others? And "Are you thirsty? Hungry?" And "I love you. Do you know how much I love you?"

Her tail wagged wildly. It seemed it would never stop.

The Lassie tin might be empty, but we kept a three-month supply of kibble in the cupboard. Misty wouldn't care that there were no leftovers to spread on top of her meal.

"Let's get you a fresh drink," I said, realizing at that moment that I was thirsty and hungry, too. The hot chocolate and doughnut at Clovers had been this morning. Or years ago, depending on your perspective.

Suddenly, my home was my home again.

In the kitchen, I poured fresh water in a bowl for Misty and opened a bag of kibble. She lapped water frantically and licked the empty bowl. As she gulped down her food, I opened the refrigerator and surveyed my choices. They were grim. No leftover food. No lunch meat. Not even salad makings, but a package of cheese with a spread of mold on one end that could be cut off.

Beggars can't be choosers. I wiped dust off the teapot, wondering how long it had been since I'd used it.

A day?

As the water boiled, I glanced at the calendar. It was still August, but the picture of a pair of collie puppies in the arms of a vintage child was unfamiliar, and...Dear Lord, it was two years later than it should be!

Fortified by bites of cheese, possibly my least favorite food, I sat on the porch and made a plan. Rather, I revised a plan I'd considered earlier, before I knew that Misty was going to join me in this mixed-up world. I would return to Huron Court and, holding tight to Misty, hope I'd travel in time again.

It had worked for Linnea Wilmott.

Perhaps too well. I didn't want to land in the wrong decade, or worse, the wrong century, but what other option was available to me? Stay here and wait for a husband who wouldn't return?

Misty had eaten her full and lay at my feet, with one paw pressing heavily on my shoe. The sooner we started, the better.

It occurred to me that this day seemed longer than it should be, every hour feeling more like two than one. Well, why not, since time had lost its way?

~ * ~

I didn't encounter a single soul on the way to Huron Court, which gave the walk the surreal feel of a dream. All down Sagramore Lake Road, at the lake, on the beach—no one was out and about enjoying one of the last days of summer.

The silence persisted, and it appeared that the earth and sky had acquired muted colors. Mauve, pale pink, beige, and soft gray. Colors of a dream.

Misty walked on a leash, happily sniffing every plant and inanimate object in our path. I wasn't going to take the chance of our being separated again. To her, this was an ordinary walk. She couldn't know how much depended on it.

I wished desperately for a sign of normalcy. A glimpse of a fox in wilderness, a deer leaping in my path. Birdsong. Anything.

There was nothing. Only a world of green that went on and on and on until I reached the first of the McMansions. As I was still in the future, that meant Autumn's trail would be all but impossible to find without the fallen branch barring the entrance.

Look for the patch of yellow wildflowers. The one landmark.

When I found it, I would have to blaze my own trail. But how would I find the exact spot where I'd fallen out of my time?

It seemed I'd set myself an impossible task, but if I wanted to go home, I had to do the impossible.

Twenty-eight

Finding the trail was my first problem, complicated by the profusion of wildflowers that splashed the edge of the woods with color. On closer inspection, however, none of them resembled lilies.

At last, I found what was almost certainly the trail with wild lily lookalikes shaded by a massive tree that might have lost a branch in the past. When Misty showed an inordinate interest in the ground, I decided this was indeed the place where I'd entered the woods earlier today.

No, two years ago.

No longer a trail but deep woodland, it was thoroughly uninviting. Undaunted, I stepped into the underbrush and let Misty take the lead. Pushing aside all kinds of plant life, I tried to walk in a straight line as I had before.

It was cool in the woods, as was to be expected. So cool, it was almost chilly. Unnaturally so?

A slight disturbance in the air hinted of change on the way. Rain?

The drops fell without further warning, first a few, then a torrent of stinging, icy...snowflakes!

I pulled on Misty's leash.

"Stay close to me!"

Snow falling in summer could only mean that a shift in time was imminent.

I felt Misty's leash slip out of my hand and grabbed for her fur. I missed and felt a sudden pounding on top of my head, a dizzying, sickening sensation. I closed my eyes against the pain and reached again for Misty but held only air.

"Hey, Jennet! What the heck?"

The snow was gone. Misty was gone. Annica knelt beside me, leaves stuck to her bright hair. She was tugging at something on the ground, pulling it free in a shower of dirt. A long, thick vine covered with red berries.

"You warn me about tripping, and here you're the one who trips."

"My head hurts," I murmured.

"Did you hit it when you fell?"

"I don't remember."

She helped me up. I stood, unsteady on my feet. My head was throbbing.

"Where's Misty?"

"Yikes, you did hit your head. She's at home. Where else would she be?"

"She was with me."

"No, Jennet. Not today. Let's hurry. That mist looks positively lethal, and it's getting closer."

I saw it then: wispy tendrils rising from the earth, swirling through the trees.

My wish had been granted. We were back where we'd been before the vine had grabbed hold of my foot, running from the mist. My visit to the future had been thankfully brief.

"I need to take something for my headache," I said.

~ * ~

Annica volunteered to drive, for which I was grateful as I felt shaky. It wasn't until we had passed the fork in Huron Court that I was able to talk.

"Back there," I said. "I traveled in time."

"How could you? You were right behind me. Then you fell."

"Yes, I fell into the future."

"It was only a few minutes."

"It was most of the day."

We were passing Sagramore Lake. I fixed my gaze on the still, familiar waters and described my stay in the future.

"Where was I all this time?" Annica asked.

"You weren't there. I didn't see anyone. I was alone. The path we were on was gone," I added. "So was the car, and there were three houses on the road."

"This was two years from now?'

"According to the calendar. Then Misty came out of the woods, and I decided to come back to the trail."

I had forgotten to mention the strange, muted hues of the future world I'd visited. Everything was brighter now. The sky was a deeper blue filled with floating white clouds, and the earth shone in multiple shades of green. What was the significance of the color change?

"It sounds like a dream," Annica said.

"But it really happened. You know what Time can do."

"Yeah, from experience. Still, you didn't disappear. Not like Brent and the girls and Linnea."

"It's a variation, then. I remember thinking I was dead. That dreadful black wreath on the door. My dogs gone, and I didn't know where Crane was. It was real and terrible."

"Brent is still missing," she said. "I'm going back to the trail tomorrow and hope the mist won't be there and, even if it is...I have a strong feeling he went that way. I have to find him."

"We will," I said. "Somehow, somewhere, we'll find all our lost ones. After all, I came home. But maybe you'd better avoid the trail."

"That's exactly where I need to be, she said.

~ * ~

Thanks to capricious Time, the rest of the day was normal. Camille was home, weeding in her flower garden. I waved to her. The dogs were crowded in the front window, barking their customary welcome. There was no black wreath on the door.

In the kitchen, the image of a running tricolor on the collie calendar accompanied the correct month and year. I opened the refrigerator and found the steaks I'd brought out of the freezer to defrost and four ears of corn. Crane would grill the steaks and I'd make a salad. I had no doubt this would happen.

It was a true blessing to be alive, and after I'd taken medication with a cup of hot tea, my headache eased up.

That evening as Crane and I lingered over dinner, I told him about my brief adventure in time. Like Annica, he said, "Are you sure it wasn't a dream?"

"I'd stake my life on it," I said.

He covered my hand with his, understanding what really frightened me. "That doesn't mean you'll die in...what was it? Two years?"

"I certainly hope not, but there was that black wreath on the door."

"That's not something I would do. Didn't you say something about not being able to meet yourself when you travel in time?" he asked.

"So they say."

"That sounds logical, I guess."

"What about the black wreath?"

He kept his hand in place. "There are lots of reasons why you found the house the way you did."

"For instance?"

"I was on duty."

"How about the dogs?"

He didn't answer.

"And the almost empty refrigerator?"

"You needed to go grocery shopping."

"If anything happened to me, would you keep the dogs?"

"They're my dogs, too," he said. "Here's what you're going to do. From now on, think about it as a bad dream. By the way, Camille would have told us if Misty went missing today."

"She was with me."

"You often said our love is forever."

I nodded. "Yes."

"Keep telling yourself that."

It was advice I was happy to take.

Twenty-nine

The following week passed without incident, and, suddenly, it was time to go back to school, for the teachers, that is. We would report the next morning, while the students would enjoy all Friday and another sun-filled weekend of vacation.

Jennifer and Molly and the dogs were still missing, but Brent had appeared at the barn this morning, oblivious of the fact that he had lost four days of his life.

He couldn't believe it.

For once, he stopped to visit us without bringing a gift bag of dog treats. The collies still fawned on him, shoving one another out of the way to nudge his empty hands. They didn't love him for his presents.

"It's Friday. Look at the *Banner*." I pointed to the date on the first page.

"That's what Annica and the guys at the barn said."

I handed him a root beer. "Drink this and calm down."

"I don't remember being away," he said. "Maybe I have a brain tumor."

"I think you tangled with our old friend, Time. It's having different effects on people."

"Did they find the girls while I was gone?"

"Not yet. I'm afraid they're stranded in time."

"We can't leave them there," he said.

"I don't know where to look, but I'm hoping they'll appear like you did."

His angst increased as I told him about my own strange hours in the future.

"Why don't I remember anything?" he asked.

He looked so bereft I longed to comfort him. But how?

"What do you remember?" I asked.

"I was brushing one of the collies. Chance."

"You were at the barn?"

"No, wait. I was on Huron Court. I wanted to see this mystery mist for myself. After that, it's all fuzzy."

That was where Doug had found Brent's vintage Plymouth parked on the verge.

"I was going to take Annica out for coffee after her shift," he said.

"Big spender."

He didn't rise to my teasing.

"Then it was morning. A beautiful morning. I stopped for pancakes at Clovers. I thought Annica was going to faint. She told me how long I'd been gone. How can that be if I don't remember?"

"It may come to you when you least expect it," I said.

And maybe it wouldn't. Time was toying with us. I had lived several hours of my own possible future while, to Annica, I never left the trail and only minutes passed. Brent had no memory of dropping out of time and what happened then. Molly and Jennifer and the dogs were…Somewhere. Not to mention Linnea Wilmott. I was dealing with a different kind of time travel. It seemed to be mutating.

"It must be true," he said at last, "unless you all joined forces to trick me. It's funny, though. Except for the few miles Doug put on the car driving it back to the barn, the mileage on the Belvedere didn't change. There's never a day when I don't drive it."

"There's your proof," I said.

"Why did I leave the keys in the ignition and walk away? I hate not knowing what I was doing."

"I'm sure you were trying to find your way back to us. And look, you did. So be of good cheer."

"There's nothing cheerful about losing days of your life." He drained the can of pop. "Can I have another one?"

"You may."

As usual, the dogs alerted me to Crane's arrival before I heard his Jeep in the driveway.

He came in, making his way through the tail-wagging welcome committee and kissed me with less ardor than usual as Brent was grinning at us.

"Welcome back, Fowler," he said. "You're supposed to be missing."

"No longer true."

"What were you up to?"

"I haven't a clue," he said.

Crane locked his gun in the cabinet and joined us at the table, by which time I had opened another root beer for him. We were silent as Brent kept trying to recall other fragments of his lost memory without success. All that remained in his mind were brushing Chance and driving to the trail.

"This trail is off limits to you two." Crane spoke in in his dictatorial deputy sheriff's voice, never a good sign. "It caused Jennet to fall and you to vanish."

Brent bristled. "Look here, Sheriff, you can't tell me what to do. I didn't vote for you."

I held back a laugh. "No one did. It doesn't work that way."

"In fact, stay away from Huron Court, both parts of it," Crane added.

He set the empty can on the counter. "Just in case you two decide to hunt for Jennifer and Molly. We're all looking for them."

"If you don't find them soon, they'll miss school," I said.

"We're doing all we can."

"Now that I'm back, I can help," Brent said.

"No." I knew he'd feel that way, but it was too dangerous with Time lurking in the background waiting to displace us. "We don't want to lose you again."

"Listen to Jennet," Crane said.

I held fast to the notion that one day the girls would walk back into the present with Ginger and Autumn.

It could happen.

~ * ~

It looked certain that Jennifer and Molly were going to miss the beginning of the school year. I couldn't help thinking about them the next morning as Leonora and I walked down a pristine, silent hall to our classrooms. The girls had been looking forward to beginning new classes and reconnecting with friends they hadn't seen all summer.

They still had a weekend to come back. A weekend and a day.

"It's like we never left," Leonora said as I unlocked my door.

I nodded. "The summer flew by. It always does."

My job at present was to turn a long disused room into a welcoming place. Textbooks liberated from the musty closet, fresh construction paper on the bulletin boards, paper leaves ordered from a catalog.

The view of the wooded acreage owned by the district and home to a herd of deer was enticing, and the windows were clean. The entire room was immaculate with a lingering scent of lemony furniture polish. All it needed was fresh air.

One by one I opened the windows, thoughts of untoward disappearances and time travel slowly receding in the demands of the moment. Readying my room for an avalanche of teenagers was something I could do.

Thirty

I woke the next morning to brilliant sunshine and a resolve to make my last free weekend memorable. It was already warm in the house, unusually so for September. I was alone in the bedroom, and the enticing scent of bacon wafted up from the kitchen.

Darn! I wanted to be the first one up.

In the kitchen, the dogs were crunching their morning biscuits and Crane was taking the box of pancake mix out of the cupboard. Time for me to take over. He surrendered the box without comment and poured coffee for us.

"It's going to be hot today," he said. "A good day to take it easy. What are you going to do?"

I took a second to think about it. Temptation reared its head. Autumn's trail. The mist. The summer's mysteries that remained unsolved. The days had dwindled down to a precious few.

But I wasn't about to venture within a mile of Huron Court. I'd never understood the intrepid Gothic heroine who strolls blithely into danger knowing full well she is courting disaster but not caring.

I didn't understand her, but in truth, often emulated her.

Still, I recalled Linnea fretting about not being able to report to school after Christmas recess. I couldn't let something like that happen to me.

But failure is a heavy burden to shoulder. I'd had to leave Linnea stranded in the past or future. I hadn't brought Autumn home. Because of my encouraging Jennifer and Molly to join in the search for her, I'd left them open to unknown peril.

How could I ignore all that and return to teaching English as usual at Marson High School?

Crane was sipping coffee, waiting for an answer.

"I'd like to do all my favorite things while I have plenty of leisure time."

"Like?"

"Visit Lucy, talk to Annica, go to the library. I've hardly seen Miss Eidt all summer. Oh, and play with the dogs until they get tired."

"Do it all then," he said, "but don't drive down Huron Court."

"You issued your edict yesterday. Loud and clear."

"I just gave you good advice."

"And I'm going to take it. Promise."

Naturally it never occurred to me to do otherwise.

~ * ~

The gold Zodiac charms on Lucy's favorite bracelet jingled as she poured boiling water in my teacup and stirred the leaves vigorously. Sky tilted her head and watched as Lucy's long black scarf brushed against the plate of cookies.

"I was going to call you today," she said. "I woke with one of my premonitions. Linnea Wilmott was standing by my bedside trying to communicate with me. But she wasn't making any sound. Either that or I couldn't hear her."

"That's a scary way to wake up."

"I should say. I thought I was dreaming, especially when she faded into the background, but her feelings of loss and hopelessness stayed behind. I sense that she needs help, and time is running out."

"That's a curious concept," I said, thinking of sand in an hourglass drifting slowly downward.

When I thought about Linnea, I saw her dressed comfortably in period clothes spinning books in her time travel series on an old typewriter. Lucy had a different visualization.

"Before I was fully awake, I remembered a dream I had of a woman in a barren landscape," she said. "There were hardly any trees, only rutted ground and sky."

"That must be the distant future, after a war. Time is sending its victims all over the place."

"All she wanted was to go back to 1998 and change her future," Lucy said.

"Apparently it was too much to ask for."

Time wasn't a benevolent being who could bestow favors at will.

Lucy sighed. "I don't know how I can help her. She must think I can."

"If I could help anyone, it would be Jennifer and Molly," I said. "It's not that I don't sympathize with Linnea, but playing with time was her choice. The girls were just trying to find Linnea's dog."

Sky nudged my hand, her eyes on the cookies.

"Don't you think something else might have happened?" Lucy asked. "Like they were abducted?"

"It's more likely that they went looking for Autumn on Huron Court and were whisked out of time. I see a little group. Two girls and two dogs. They say there's safety in numbers."

"That's not always true," Lucy pointed out. "But back to Linnea. If she's trying to communicate with me, like she did with the garden statue, she may try again. I'll be watching for anything untoward."

I drained my cup. "Let's see if the tea leaves have anything relevant to say."

Lucy studied the formations in my teacup carefully, holding the cup toward the light as if in search of alternate interpretations. My heart sank at the expression on her face.

"What?"

"I see a scene similar to the one from my dream. There's a desolate landscape and a lonely figure. It's you." She pointed to a formation that looked like a juxtaposition of dark and light leaves.

"How can you tell it's me?" I asked. "Couldn't it be Linnea?"

"It's your cup," Lucy said. "Your fortune."

"How can you see all that?" I asked.

"Practice," Lucy said. "And a talent I've been blessed, or cursed, with. The end result is that you may be heading for danger. Again."

"I'll try to head the other way."

"Easier said than done," Lucy said. "Remember, the messages in the teacup aren't set in stone. Believing them is your choice."

"I'm going to play it safe and give Huron Court a wide berth," I said. "The only mist I want to see will be outside my window."

Thirty-one

I needed a respite from Lucy's gloom and doom and knew I could find it at Clovers, with a lime cooler close at hand and the good company of my partner-in-crime, Annica, whose sunny disposition would have returned now that Brent was safe.

An hour later, Annica set my dream drink in front of me. Her eyes sparkled with secret triumph. "Alethea strikes again," she announced.

"You don't seem upset. What did she do?"

"She came to Clovers for lunch and started making jokes about runaway grooms. Somehow she heard that Brent was missing but not that he'd come back."

"How did you respond?"

"I took her order with a smile and didn't react to her nonsense."

"How frustrating for her."

"She was practically breathing fire. I've never seen her at Clovers. I'm sure her only reason for coming today was to harass me."

"You didn't let her succeed. If that's the best she can do, you don't have anything to worry about."

"But from her point of view, her mission fell apart. She'll be waiting in the wings with something new."

"And you'll be ready for her."

I swirled my spoon through the mint-colored froth and savored the perfect blend of tart and sweet.

This is the last lime cooler of the summer, I thought. If only Annica would divulge her secret recipe!

"What are we going to do about Jennifer and Molly?" Annica asked.

"Everyone is still searching for them, but it isn't looking good."

She tapped her engagement ring fondly. "I feel guilty being so happy when we don't know where the girls are or if we'll ever see them again."

"You deserve your happiness," I said, "and they'll come home. Don't ask me how I know it, but they will."

Those perennially happy, enterprising girls in their Dogfinders shirts with Ginger and Linnea's Autumn whom I'd never set eyes on. They couldn't simply fall off the face of the planet.

"There's no point in cruising down Huron Court, I suppose," Annica said.

"None at all, unless we want to take an impromptu trip in time. I don't."

"Then all we can do is wait."

The waiting game was Time's favorite diversion. It wasn't mine.

~ * ~

All of a sudden, the little restaurant buzzed with activity. People fairly streamed through the door to the ringing of the clover wind chimes. They soon claimed all the available tables and booths.

"I have to go to work," Annica said and glided toward the counter.

As I finished my drink, I took one last look at the woods of Crispian Road. The next time I saw them, the leaves would be changing color. I'd have less free time and by then I would know whether my classes would be pleasant or challenging or downright impossible.

We could travel in time if we were lucky, or unlucky, but we couldn't see the future.

~ * ~

The old white Victorian-turned-library drowsed in the warmth of the midday sun, the trees on the grounds rustling in a light breeze while the last of summer's vibrant flowers clung to life.

From a cushion on her chair, Miss Eidt's cat, Blackberry, kept a jewel-eyed watch on all comers but didn't move, giving a fair impression of a feline lawn ornament.

Nonetheless, I sent a brief greeting her way and opened the door, noting that Miss Eidt had anticipated the new season with a wreath of blue asters and trailing purple ribbons.

Inside, Miss Eidt looked serene as ever, dressed in a pale lavender suit with matching nail polish that caught the sparkle of her engagement diamond. She sat at her desk, gazing out at her domain, a box of books at her elbow. One could hear the proverbial pin drop.

The library was without a doubt the most peaceful place in Foxglove Corners. None of the patrons would dare cause a disturbance or defy her authority or litter the floor. The library was as far removed from a high school classroom as possible and the perfect place to while away a lazy September Saturday.

I tried to imagine myself gazing out at my domain in Marston High School with the same serenity. It didn't work.

"Hi, Miss Eidt," I said, glancing at the box. "More new arrivals?"

"They're from the attic. Debbie and I finally finished our spring house cleaning."

I lifted a pristine copy of the rarely seen *Beverly Gray at the World's Fair* and held it reverently. A collector would be thrilled to own this volume. An ordinary reader, not so much.

"It was my own," Miss Eidt said. "I always believed in treating my books well. But most of these won't go on the shelves. We're thinking of having a sale later in the month."

"Could I look them over first?" I asked.

"You may. If you see something you like, feel free to take it."

Who could turn down such an offer?

Miss Eidt and I had similar tastes in books. One slender volume, complete with dust cover, looked as if it had arrived directly from the publisher. The title, *The Secret of the White Fog*, caught my immediate attention as did the name of the author, June Summers.

I felt certain I was holding another book by Linnea Wilmott.

Thirty-two

The copyright date was September, 1937, which suggested that Linnea had traveled to the wrong year again, but was apparently supporting herself by writing books under the name of June Summers. At least that was my assumption. Or...Another idea occurred to me. Had she been fated to live out her life in the past, aging as the decades changed? In that case, she would be dead by now. I didn't want to believe that.

It would be helpful if the cover contained a short biography of the author or even better a picture.

I closed the book and studied the dust cover. The scene resembled Huron Court in late fall with an extravagance of gold and russet leaves draped in white fog. In the distance I could make out a majestic blue Victorian house.

What was the secret?

"June Summers is the penname of our missing time traveler, Linnea Wilmott," I said. "I'll definitely take this book."

Miss Eidt held out her hand. "May I see it, please?"

I handed it to her and turned back to the box hoping to find more treasures. When I looked up again, I was surprised to see a puzzled look on her face.

"This isn't mine," she said.

"Are you sure?"

She had opened the book to the first chapter and obviously read the opening paragraphs. "I'm positive."

Miss Eidt was a voracious reader, but in spite of its pristine appearance, *The Secret of the White Fog* was several decades old. "How can you possibly remember every book you read over the years?" I asked.

"I just do. Besides..." She flipped back to the first pages. "I always write my name in my books. These pages are all blank."

I sighed. Did every breakthrough have to come with a new mystery?

"It looks good," I said and pushed the box closer to her. "How about the others?"

She examined the contents quickly. "They all look familiar. They're mine. Every one except for *The Secret of the White Fog*. I never saw that book."

"I don't understand," I said.

"Neither do I. This is my box. It was in my attic. But where this book came from, I can't imagine."

She twisted her long rope of pearls, a familiar nervous gesture.

"Let me go back a little. When I decided to turn my family home into a library, I took my favorite things to the new house and packed everything else away. My cousin, Ellen, helped me. Most of the books went up to the attic. I always planned to sort them but never found the time. Those were hectic days, and after that, it was out of sight, out of mind."

I could think of one explanation, although it was as far out as it could be.

"Could Linnea herself have left a copy of her book in your house?"

"Possibly. A lot of painters and handymen were coming and going in those days, and I even employed a cleaning service. But why would she do that?"

"As one of her weird messages? Like the one she left under the garden statue?"

On the surface that would seem unlikely as there was little chance Miss Eidt would find the book, much less know what it meant. If Linnea were going to leave a message, it seemed she would have found a way to make sure Lucy or I saw it. We were both frequent visitors to the library. Even so...

I shuffled through the pages, willing a hidden paper to fall out. Nothing did. Not even a bookmark.

"This doesn't make any sense," I said, "but I'll read it as soon as I get home. Maybe the message is in the story. Possibly it contains a call for help and a way to bring her home."

That would be nice, but I didn't believe it.

"This is so exciting," Miss Eidt said. "To think a time traveler left her book in my house, and Ellen and I just moved it up to the attic without realizing its significance."

If that was what had happened. It sounded improbable, but at the moment I couldn't think of any other explanation.

~ * ~

At home, I rushed through my chores, planned our dinner, took the dogs for a walk, and settled down in my rocker with *The Secret of the White Fog*.

Fog, not mist. There was a difference. Still...

Linnea had penned a mystery that could easily have been reprinted and marketed as a Gothic in the sixties. It was a thinly veiled time travel without the machine. The further I read, the more convinced I was that June Summers was our lost Linnea Wilmott.

The setting was a clear giveaway. Within walking distance of Holiday Circle (Huron Court?), Lake Indigo drew dozens of sunbathers in the summer months. The area was rural with a few isolated estates and plenty of woods.

The heroine, Aurelia, running away from a Halloween party and a lecherous date, found herself on a lonely, twisting road. The only house in sight was a blue Victorian. Violet Randall's house with a change in color?

Aurelia was afraid she was being followed. Then a new menace threatened her.

The fog came without warning. It dropped down from the sky, rose up from the ground, and surrounded her, shutting her off from the rest of the world. Someone walked behind her, hidden from view by the white wall that slowly took shape around her. The fog thickened and touched her with icy, slimy claws. She tumbled over an obstacle in the road, also hidden, and fell heavily forward on the hard ground. As she lay there, stunned, she heard a sound...

"Jennet!"

Crane's voice broke through the spell cast by June Summers'/Linnea Wilmott's scene. I hadn't heard him come inside, hadn't even heard the dogs barking.

"You don't often get lost in a book," he said.

"This isn't just any book. I'm pretty sure Linnea Wilmott is the author. She's writing about Huron Court, only she calls it Holiday Circle."

"Did you come across anything important?" he asked.

I closed the book, now firmly back into my real life, the one where my roast was probably overdone.

"Not yet," I said.

Thirty-three

In my dream I was running down a misty road in a desperate attempt to escape from a menace which I couldn't see—had never seen, even though I heard his (its) labored breathing and sensed that something frightful was close behind me.

If I couldn't see it, it couldn't see me.

A strange white fog lay heavily over the ground. I could hide in its white folds. Or turn into the woods and take refuge among the thickly spaced trees until the threat passed. But then what? Where was I going anyway?

I couldn't remember.

I stopped to catch my breath. Should I keep moving or hide in the woods? That was when I heard the dog barking.

Waking was painful. I was breathing as heavily as if I had been running for my life. The top of my nightgown was damp. It was still early, still dark. Crane slept on, but one of the dogs was barking downstairs, and Misty pranced alongside the bed whimpering nervously.

For a moment I couldn't remember what day it was.

I glanced at Crane, who was still asleep, and hushed her. The dogs rarely barked at night unless some nocturnal creature ventured too close to the house.

Whatever the disturbance, I always investigated. Pushing the covers aside, I recoiled at the blast of cold air. Turning on the hall light, I followed Misty downstairs.

Candy was wide awake, her paws on the chair by the window, barking frantically at something I wouldn't be able to see.

"It's all right, girl, calm down," I said, which had no effect on my rebel collie.

I decided to stay up and was sitting at the table waiting for the coffee to brew and planning breakfast when Crane appeared incredibly bright and handsome, already dressed for a day of patrol, as he always is in the morning.

"What's all the barking about?" he asked.

"It's Candy," I said. "Who else? She probably saw a deer. Maybe a coyote."

Nothing untoward for a country dweller. At any rate, the creature was gone, and Candy's attention turned to food which she knew would be forthcoming. She stationed herself in a sit beside Crane's empty chair.

Another morning, I thought. Please let something good happen today.

~ * ~

Everyone was looking for Jennifer and Molly. The members of Dogfinders, including the search-and-rescue dog, were now searching for their young co-founders, along with the girls' classmates, friends, and families. With so many people combing the Foxglove Corners wilderness, it was inconceivable that they remained missing. Two young girls and two Lassie dogs. They had to be somewhere.

Of course, no one knew our suspicion that they had fallen into Time's trap.

Reports of occasional sightings found their way into the news. Some seemed outrageous, especially the few that dealt with one girl and not the other. Wherever they were, I doubted Jennifer and Molly would allow themselves to be separated, and certainly they would keep the dogs with them. If possible.

A waitress in a Maple Creek restaurant claimed a girl resembling Molly had ordered four cheeseburgers, two plain and two with everything.

"You must be hungry" the waitress had said.

The reply: "Two are for our dogs."

Hence the customer must have been Molly.

Look for the missing girls in Maple Creek.

Then a farmer reported that two brown and white dogs 'just like Lassie' had been stealing ripe tomatoes from his vines.

A witness had sworn he'd seen both girls riding out of town in a convertible driven by a bearded man in black.

I had no faith in these tales. But I did wonder if the girls had sufficient funds to provide for themselves and two dogs. Like Linnea, they hadn't planned to be snatched out of their rightful time.

The Dogfinders took up a collection and offered a reward for information leading to the girls' safe return. Nobody mentioned recovering bodies. At least not in my hearing.

"You're the expert, Jennet," Brent said one evening while we sat at the kitchen table talking about the girls. They had now missed three days of school. "What do we do next? And don't say 'Wait'."

"I'm no expert, and I have no idea. I wish I did."

"We have to bring them home."

"We're searching," Crane said with a testy note in his voice. He had responded to that question multiple times.

While he didn't discount my 'lost in time' theory, he believed they might have been abducted and taken out of the state.

All four of them?

"Why?" I'd asked him. "They couldn't have any enemies. There's no ransom note. Do you think it was a random kidnapping, or they fell into the hands of a psychopath?"

Two girls. Two dogs.

"Both are possible," was his reply.

"The mist got them," Brent said. "That damn mist. It took Linnea Wilmott. It tried to take you, but you were too smart for it. For all I know, it took me. I still don't remember anything about the time I went missing. Two helpless girls were easier to deal with."

I let that last part go. In my opinion, the girls were anything but helpless, and the dogs were collies.

"Wild speculation doesn't help," Crane said.

Brent bristled. "What does?"

"More lemonade, Fowler?" Crane asked. "Or would you like something stronger?"

He'd only taken one swallow of my lemonade and proceeded to glare at it.

"This stuff is stronger than I am," he said. "Could I have some sugar, Jennet?"

I passed him the sugar bowl and watched him stir three teaspoons into his drink. For me, the lemonade was perfect. I always made it the same way. Brent simply wanted to complain about something he could change.

"Since I've been back, I checked out that trail twice," he said. "I didn't see a speck of mist. It was clear blue sky all the way."

"Time doesn't want you. You're too tough."

Which was an unkind rejoinder. Brent was genuinely baffled. Crane was frustrated but determined to do everything in his power to solve the case. People we cared about had vanished, and I couldn't see a happy ending for anyone.

"Why don't we all get together—Annica, Lucy, you and I, and even the sheriff here if he can find the time. Since you think the mist caused the problem, we'll go up and down that trail until we see a mist and force it to give up the girls."

"You should be thanking your lucky stars you returned safe and sound," Crane said. "Go chasing after a mist if you want to, but leave Jennet and her friends out of it."

"Let Jennet decide for herself," Brent countered.

"Let's think of another plan," I said.

Thirty-four

After Brent left, I finished reading *The Secret of the White Fog*. The secret appeared to be a miniature apparatus encased in a cameo-like amulet that Aurelia found when she stumbled over a dislodged rock in the road.

In examining it, she inadvertently touched a trigger that sent her a hundred years into the past. Thus, thanks to a time machine of sorts, she evaded her pursuer.

This led to new problems. Where was she and could she find her way back home? The weather was changing. Dark clouds promised rain.

While seeking a place to shelter from a sudden downpour, she met Richard, the tall dark, and handsome master of Mist House, who had his own issues. As she now possessed the means to transport herself back to the present, she could leave Mist House at any time but elected to stay in the past with Richard for whom she felt a strong attraction.

With its familiar Gothic pattern, this book couldn't be more different from the Linda Welsch series, but I suspected both were written by Linnea Wilmott. Occasionally I came across a word which she had used frequently at Lucy's tea party. Also she described the pink

Victorian, now called Mist House, as being set in a wildflower meadow which didn't exist until the house had burned and Brent purchased the scorched land.

Still, she was obviously writing about Huron Court, making good use of poetic license, and the themes rang true: being lost, attempting to find the road that would take her home.

I closed the book with a sigh. It was no help whatsoever as I couldn't scour the roads of Foxglove Corners looking for a cameo-like amulet with a time machine inside. The device was undoubtedly a figment of the author's imagination.

Time didn't need a clever gadget to operate. I was back to square one, and the girls were still missing.

~ * ~

The next morning a thick white fog filled the air on and around Jonquil Lane. I stood at the bedroom window gazing at about eight feet of our property and, beyond that, a solid white wall. The lane and Camille's yellow Victorian might not have existed.

This, I felt certain, was a natural fog that shouldn't inspire undue apprehension. No matter. A warning bell began to ring in my mind. Beware of fog wherever you find it.

Fortunately, it was Sunday, and Leonora and I didn't have to drive to Oakpoint. Now I'd better go outside with the dogs, lest one of them wander too far. One of them? Only Candy would be so reckless.

At present, everyone in the house except Misty was still sleeping. I had unwittingly communicated my anxiety to her. She leaned on me, and I felt her tremble. This wouldn't do. We all needed breakfast.

I slipped into a bright red dress for a murky day and joined the other dogs in the kitchen where I passed out biscuits and poured fresh water. As I did every morning.

As soon as I opened the side door, I heard the barking. It sounded like the distinctive bark of a collie, high pitched and insistent. As a matter of fact, it sounded like one of mine, but no. They were all here circling me, tails wagging, full of energy after a long sleep.

Misty was the only dog to react to the mystery barker. The others showed no inclination to run into the fog but stayed close to the house.

I stood still, my hand on the doorknob, listening. Yes, that was definitely a collie. At first, I thought the barking came from the unfinished construction site. Then it seemed nearer, as close as the woods across the lane. In the next second, it appeared to be further away, almost inaudible, and now I couldn't tell which direction it was coming from.

How strange. But it was too early in the day for strange.

I called the dogs inside and reached for the iron skillet and the eggs. I would make Crane a hearty country breakfast and watch the fog burn away from inside the house. I didn't like the feeling of being encased in unyielding white, but my kitchen was cozy and familiar and safe.

Stay inside. Stay safe.

"We're going to be busy today," Crane announced as he entered the kitchen. "Speeders and fog are a bad combination."

I couldn't imagine anyone driving fast in these conditions. Or driving at all if it could be avoided.

"Did you hear a dog barking a few minutes ago?" I asked.

"One of ours?"

"No, but a collie. I'd know a collie's bark anywhere."

"It's quiet enough now."

That was true, but only for the moment as Candy gave a pathetic cry designed to transfer a piece of bacon from the grill to her mouth. She went so far as to place her paws on the counter.

I redirected her attention to an unnoticed biscuit that had somehow found its way to the middle of the floor, under the table.

"Be careful today, Crane," I said. "Don't take any chances."

He kissed the top of my head. "I'm always careful, honey. You can't do anything more than that."

~ * ~

The sun was in no hurry to appear, but by nine o'clock I could see the yellow Victorian. It appeared to be swimming in a sea of fog, and somewhere out there in the vast, unseen wilderness, the dog began to bark again. As before, only Misty was aware of the disturbance. She whined and paced at the side door and, gradually my mind made a connection.

Collie barking. Dog in distress. Autumn.

I opened the door and called her name. For a moment, my voice was the only sound in the silent, white world. Then the barking resumed, definitely coming from the direction of the abandoned construction site.

Grabbing a handful of treats from the Lassie tin, I ventured a few steps away from the house and called again. A brush of warm velvet against my leg told me that Misty had followed me. I took hold of her collar and called Autumn again. This time I was rewarded by a glimpse of a sable and white collie wreathed in streamers of fog and so close I could almost take a few more steps and touch her.

I knew a brief moment of exultation. Autumn had left the woods of Huron Court in search of human contact even as we were searching for her. She must be aware that eight of her kind lived in the house, perhaps even that I had tasty treats to give to a good dog.

"Autumn!" I called. "Come!"

At my call, the collie vanished in moving rolls of fog. Misty gave an impatient little whimper.

"All right," I said. "Just a little way. Stay with me."

Autumn began to bark again. It grew louder and more frantic. I walked toward the sound, willing her to show herself again.

"I have liver treats!"

But something was wrong. With every step I took, I felt as if I were sinking into a dream landscape from which all familiar landmarks had been devoured and all sound silenced. Even the barking, which was now so faint I might be imagining it.

Misty whined and pressed her body close to mine. I tightened my hand around her collar.

Stop! Go back!

Just one more step. I was still on our property, still on the far side of the fog bank. It would be one hundred percent safe.

Wouldn't it?

Thirty-five

"Jennet?"

The voice came out of the fog, soft, tremulous, familiar.

Jennifer?

I looked over my shoulder, aghast to find that my house was no longer visible. How had I ventured so far into the fog while telling myself all the time to take only a few steps?

Or was the fog thickening? Expanding?

I still held Misty's collar. She was unhappy, wanting to be free, but I persisted. I couldn't afford to be separated from her, especially not now that the strangeness had become grim reality.

"Jennet! Over here!"

"Jennifer! Over where? I can't see you."

"I'm right here. I need help."

But the voice faded, and I didn't hear it again. The entire world, rather what I could perceive of it, had turned white. It was in my best interest to retrace my steps and return to the safety of my home.

And leave Jennifer and the collie out here in the fog?

Well, I couldn't connect with either of them under the circumstances. If Jennifer could find me, she could find the house.

Coward!

No, realist. The fog made it impossible to find that which I couldn't see. The silence was absolute and sinister. I wished I had Misty's leash, but I hadn't counted on her following me. At any rate, I couldn't hold on to her any longer.

"We're going back to the house," I said and, removing my hand from her collar, rubbed the dull ache away.

Back to the house…We started walking, Misty staying close to my side. Only it shouldn't take so long. Could I have passed it? It wasn't likely. I had walked in a straight line into the fog and hadn't made a single turn. And yet…Where was the house?

Keep walking.

Gradually the fog began to dissolve around me. *Finally*. The house came into view, each graceful green line distinct. Across the lane the yellow Victorian shimmered in the weakling sun.

Camille was outside, kneeling in her garden, tossing weeds into a box. Holly and Twister lay on the porch watching her. The sunshine gave the abundant black-eyed Susans and purple coneflowers a cheery shine.

"Good morning, Camille," I said. "Your flowers are gorgeous. I only have a few in bloom."

Ordinarily she would offer to pick a bouquet for me when she was done weeding. She didn't look up but tossed a tall thistle toward the box and missed. I left it where it fell.

"Did you hear the dog barking earlier?" I asked. "It was a collie. They have such a distinctive sound."

She picked up a trowel and raked dirt over the hole where the thistle had grown.

What in the world was wrong? Had Camille suddenly lost her hearing? Surely she could see me in her peripheral vision and could hear Misty making a noisy beeline for Holly and Twister.

"Camille?"

She didn't answer or react in any way.

Could she possibly be upset with me for some unknown reason? My first friend in Foxglove Corners, my kind and loving aunt by marriage, always so quick to lend a sympathetic ear or a helping hand?

That didn't seem possible, but she continued to clear her flowerbed, continued to ignore me.

Aware of rising panic, I said, "Camille, what's wrong?"

Because something was.

I touched her arm lightly and said her name again.

She never took her eye off the ground, never stopped pulling weeds.

Suddenly I knew. She wasn't aware that I was standing close to her. She hadn't felt my light touch. And Misty?

I glanced at the porch. Twister and Holly gave no indication that Misty was greeting them with wagging tail and raucous barking. Their eyes were fastened on Camille. It was as if she were engaged in the most fascinating occupation in the world; as if in the next instant she would pull a bone out of the ground. To them, Misty and I were invisible.

Accepting reality is not the same as understanding it. I only knew that Time had yanked me out of my ordained place in the universe, even though I had gone nowhere near Huron Court. Not only that. Time had stolen my body, or rather, my visibility.

I looked across the lane to where my house sat in a backdrop of wispy streamers of white, the last of the fog.

What would I find there?

Leaving Camille to her task, I crossed the lane and opened the side door to unheralded silence. No collies rushed to greet me or Misty. But all was as I'd left it, the table cleared, dishes washed and put away, the orange chiffon cake I'd baked last night on the counter in its metal holder.

"Where is everybody?" I called.

Misty whined. She'd been whining a lot lately. Her best friends had ignored her. Her mistress was clearly agitated, and now the rest of the pack had failed to welcome her home.

"Halley, Candy... Ah, there's Sky. Come, girl."

The gentle blue merle padded quietly into the kitchen, lapped water, and stretched out under the oak table, her favorite safe place in the house.

Good Lord. Sky hadn't seen me either. Nor Misty.

My anxiety grew as I moved through the house, finding each of my collies, none of them responsive, until I came to our bedroom where Halley liked to sleep in the doorway.

My precious black collie. She was with me from the beginning, in Oakpoint during the tornado, before I came to Foxglove Corners and met Crane. I reached down to pet her. I thought she turned her head toward me but couldn't be sure.

She laid her head on her paws and closed her eyes.

How much more evidence did I need that the world I'd known was gone? Or more accurately, that I was gone from the world, at least in corporeal form.

I faced the worst of all possibilities. Had I died while walking in the fog? Was I a ghost haunting my own home?

I didn't think so. I would remember a sudden blinding pain or losing consciousness.

This experience was like that other horrible time when I'd come home to find that two years had passed in my brief absence, that houses had been built and sold and moved into in that time, and that the people I cared about had inexplicably vanished.

It wasn't the same, though. It was more like I had fallen between time. I wasn't in the past or the future and certainly not in the present.

How was that possible?

Whatever had happened, I had lost them all—my husband and my dogs; my house and my life.

A deadly coldness gripped my heart and spread throughout my body. I had to fix this appalling development and couldn't do that by panicking.

Crane would come home tonight but he wouldn't be able to see me or hear me or respond to my touch. He wouldn't know what had happened. I couldn't bear to be in the same room with Crane if he wasn't aware of my presence.

I could still cook dinner for him and leave it on the stove; I could feed the dogs. Couldn't I? And I could drive. Or would possible observers see a car moving on the road without a person behind the wheel? One of those new driverless cars.

What if they did?

I had a few options, none of them palatable. I could wait for the horror to reverse itself, perhaps for the mysterious fog to return. Or I could go back to Huron Court where Time's motion was unstable. At present, I couldn't see an alternative.

Thirty-six

Before I dashed off to Huron Court, I needed to be certain that the possible outcome was worth the risk. I remembered Linnea Wilmott's determination to cruise up and down the road in the hope of driving back to the year 1998. Ever since, to my knowledge, she had been hopscotching through time. By now, she must be desperate to return to the present, which might not be possible.

That could happen to me.

It might be wiser to wait for the fog to return. If I strolled into it, would I be restored to the time when I could still be seen? Would I hear Jennifer's voice again and perhaps encounter her or Molly? If so, the three of us might be able to accomplish what one couldn't alone.

But what if the fog didn't re-form?

Misty's soft whimper reminded me that I wasn't alone as long as I had her by my side.

You have two options. Choose one.

After hasty deliberation, I decided to take a chance and return to Huron Court. The next decision was easier. Should I drive or walk?

With a last, longing look at my kitchen and Sky asleep under the table, I attached Misty's leash to her collar and grabbed my shoulder bag. "Let's go for a ride," I said.

The day was early autumn perfection with a bright warm sun, clear air, and no room for strangeness. A good omen for a successful mission, or so I hoped.

I opened the car door, and Misty jumped into the back. All right. The die was cast. Checking first to see that the driveway was free of wildlife, I turned the key in the ignition.

Nothing. The sickening silence of a car that refused to start in spite of multiple attempts. Fate must be telling me that I had to walk to Huron Court. So be it.

I led Misty back outside. "We'll make it a walk instead."

Sagramore Lake was crowded with swimmers and sunbathers taking advantage of one of the last summery days. As I led Misty on a zigzagging path between people on beach blankets who were unaware of my passing, a green ball sailed through the air, followed by a screaming little boy.

What would he think if an invisible hand (mouth) took possession of his toy?

I didn't care to find out.

We left the lake and walked resolutely toward Huron Court. The season was suddenly more advanced in this area, with leaves of crimson and gold and russet whirling through a brisk wind.

Wind? There had been no wind on the beach, but why should I be surprised? Anything was possible, and if Huron Court chose today to be a simple country road, what would I do then?

Walk on, dodge leaves, watch for white fog forming in the distance, hold onto Misty's leash with a death grip. And pray.

As we drew closer to the fork in the road, the wind gained strength. Trees swayed and groaned, and the air filled with leaves. Amid the rustling and crackling, a voice slid between its moaning.

I want to go home.

Oh, I did too. Home to the morning, to breakfast, when Crane brushed against my hand while passing me the bottle of syrup. He could see me then. Back to that time.

Help me. Please.

Jennifer's voice broke through my happy memory. She appeared to be so near she might be walking by my side. I, of course, couldn't see her, but she must be able to see me. Misty was sniffing the ground and whining. I reached through the falling leaves, but there was nothing to touch.

"Jennifer?"

I'm here. Can't you help us find the way home, Jennet?

"I wish I could. I can't help myself. Where is Molly?"

She's sick.

"And the dogs?"

I don't know.

Her voice was unnaturally soft. Soon I heard only an all-encompassing rustle and the crunching of my feet on the leaf-strewn road.

"Jennifer," I cried. "Come back."

Misty scratched furiously in the dirt, sending leaves and fresh soil into the air. A clod struck my leg and disintegrated, but Jennifer was silent.

Ahead, the fork in the road beckoned to me. Another decision. Should I take the road where I'd discovered Autumn's trail or the one where Brent's wildflowers flourished on the site of Violet Randall's pink Victorian?

The wildflower meadow, I decided, although I supposed both would be draped in the same white fog. If it appeared.

"This way," I told Misty who was still searching for the owner of the disembodied voice. "Heel."

The wind continued to strengthen. As we fought our way through the downpour of leaves, another horror gripped my mind. What if I were swept off my feet, to be blown through the air with my collie in my arms?

It was like a replay of the Oakpoint tornado. I struggled to hold on to Misty.

Don't let the wind snatch her away. Because it will. It wants to. Anything to demonstrate its power over a frail human. Anything to destroy.

I couldn't let that happen. I had to keep going. To think of Jennifer and Molly, who was sick, and the two collies who were lost again. And of Crane coming home to an empty house.

Why hadn't I left him a note?

To tell him that I was invisible? That I'd gone to the forbidden Huron Court seeking to reverse a malignant spell?

Suddenly, Misty gave a sudden surprised yelp and pulled me to the right.

What now?

Thirty-seven

Misty dove into a nest of leaves and pounced on a small object. It looked like a pork chop bone with a fair amount of meat left on it.

"No!" I cried and wrested it away from her. As I tossed it as far as I could, I realized it was still warm. Apparently recently discarded then.

Misty tugged at the leash, desperate to retrieve her treasure, and I tugged back, wondering how a half-eaten pork chop had found its way to Huron Court. That indicated the presence of another person on the road. Whether that was good or bad remained to be seen. But as long as I remained invisible, I had nothing to fear.

And nothing to gain by continuing this trek through the wind in the hope of encountering the rogue mist.

Misty was hungry, and I realized I was too. Why had I rushed away from my house so impulsively without even having a snack? It was sheer stupidity, driven by fear. From now on, I needed to stay calm and focused and, above all, to have a Plan B.

I reminded myself that just as ghosts rarely come when summoned, Huron Court would sweep me into the past or future at its own discretion. Or not at all. Judging by the last hour or so, it looked as if I were going to stay in the present, battling the monster wind.

Panic swooped down me like a rampant hawk. When night came, I would be alone on a country road, exhausted from a long walk and hungry, when I could be at home, safe and warm, and out of this horrid buffeting wind.

And invisible.

I couldn't spend the night outside. Maybe...Okay. Plan B. I could come back in the morning when the fog would possibly re-form and the wind would have died down. I wouldn't be able to communicate with Crane, though, only through notes.

Deal with that when the time comes.

I turned around and began the long walk back home through a super shower of wind-whipped leaves.

~ * ~

The wind wailed as if it were a wounded creature dying in the woods. Leaves crunched underfoot, and what was left of my energy deserted me. Misty padded along at my side, matching her pace to mine and occasionally stopped to sniff at the leaf cover for concealed mysteries.

When I felt I could go no farther, beyond the next curved I spied a splash of pink. Violet Randall's beautiful pink Victorian before it burned, before Brent and Annica planted the first wildflower seeds in the meadow.

I must have traveled in time without being aware of it. Did that mean Violet was still alive? If so, what a heaven-sent opportunity to visit her again.

But wait! I hadn't walked long enough on Huron Court to reach the wildflower meadow. Unless...Could I have gotten confused in the wild fall of leaves and passed the meadow without realizing it? I didn't think so.

Please, one mystery at a time.

I decided to accept the reality before my eyes and save questions for later. However it had happened, the pink Victorian was within reach, promising shelter even though it had an abandoned look, and no lights shone in the windows.

The wind was shrieking, determined to push me off balance. Misty pressed close to me. Any minute, the wind would take both of us and send us flying into the air. I looked for a tree to hold onto. Any tree along the roadside, as long as it was sturdy. Finding a likely willow, I grabbed the trunk and felt secure, at least for the moment.

Several more steps to safety. You can do it. No more aimless rambling. You have a goal, a place to go.

Misty, tired of fighting, lay at my feet, oblivious of the leaves collecting on her coat. After a few minutes, I tugged gently on the lead. Hope had returned. I'd traveled in time and hadn't needed the mist.

I headed for the house, coaxing Misty, who seemed reluctant to go closer.

The wind was raging. Massive branches littered on the ground, forcing me to detour around them. The wind didn't want us to find shelter. It didn't like losing victims.

We reached the porch. Misty shook herself free of leaves and looked over her shoulder, back the way we'd come. The front door was ajar. Catching my breath, I pushed it all the way open. With the howl of the wind at our heels, we stepped into the vestibule.

"Hello!" I called. "Is anyone home?"

I half expected Violet to emerge from the shadows with her collie at her heels. She would have welcomed me, I knew. But I also knew that no one was here. Violet must have already died, her ghost wandering endlessly on Huron Court.

The temperature inside was several degrees colder than it should have been, and the house was dark and full of shadows and soundless. The power had obviously failed.

I was in the living room, which was as neat as I remembered it, but small signs suggested that the people had left hurriedly and without planning: a magazine serving as a coaster for an empty mug that had once held coffee or cocoa; an unlit candle in a jar labeled 'Balsam'; a plush unicorn on the floor. A dog's toy?

In the kitchen, the refrigerator was dead. A loaf of white bread in an old-fashioned breadbox was laced with mold. A dish and spoon were rinsed and left on the counter alongside a folded towel.

But there was water. I raided the cupboard and poured some for Misty and a drink for myself. That was better, and maybe in some drawer I could find a candy bar or a package of cookies.

In spite of the unlocked door, I felt like an intruder, but if anyone appeared demanding who I was, I would be happy, for it meant that the present horror was over.

With that thought, an idea came to me.

This house would have a mirror, probably several of them. If I had a reflection, it would mean I was no longer invisible.

Thirty-eight

The mirror in the hallway was smudged, its mahogany frame coated with dust. I steeled myself to look and could have wept for joy when I saw my reflection. Pale with windblown hair, faded make-up, and the red dress I'd donned this morning for a touch of cheer. I had substance. If the mirror caught my image, so would anyone I chanced to encounter.

I reached my hand out and met my outstretched palm, while Misty touched her nose to the glass as if to greet the new dog who looked like her.

Thank God. Thank You.

The horror was over. Nothing stopped me from going home. If I left now and hurried, I could be there before Crane. In time to make dinner, to tell him what I'd been through.

"We're okay, Misty," I said, then recoiled as the truth slammed into me. Crane would still be there, but the time would be different. How long had it been since the pink Victorian had burned to the ground?

I was still trapped in the past, even if only a few years separated me from my current present to the time I'd left the house this morning.

I would have to live those years over again, those happy years. Only I wanted my life in the present returned to me.

An inner voice urged me to go back to Huron Court. Back through the wild wind and the blowing leaves. With luck I would travel in time again to the correct year.

Although that hadn't worked for Linnea.

I had nothing to lose, everything to gain. In any event, I couldn't stay in the doomed Victorian.

"Come, girl, we're going home."

I forced my gaze away from my reflection, the proof that I still had a tangible body. Leave those happy years-to-be-relived in the memory bank.

~ * ~

The wind screamed like a wolf with an arrow lodged in its heart waiting for death to release it from agony. It blew directly at me, pushing me back with every labored step I took. Leaves splattered across my face, branches broke and plunged to the ground, and an explosive sound in the distance could have been thunder or a tree crashing. I didn't think it was thunder.

Here was a new danger, being crushed by an uprooted tree, but how could I avoid it? Huron Court was all bending woods, all of it at the mercy of the wind.

The entire world filled with myriads of discordant sounds, clashing together, leaving no room for silence. No place was safe, but if I could reach Sagramore Lake, I would be out of the woods and almost home.

I left the pink Victorian far behind, dragging Misty with me, jogging until I lost my breath and a sharp pain sliced into my side. I had to stop. Just for a minute. Misty flopped down in the leaves, panting heavily.

How much further was it to the fork in the road? How many more minutes for Huron Court to work its magic?

Too far. I couldn't do this. No one could. But what was the alterative? Submit to the wind? I imagined myself forced to the ground, buried under an unending fall of leaves. And Misty...

Don't let the wind take her. Hold on!

The sudden cessation of sound caught me off guard. It was as if the wind's power had been cut off in mid-howl. Curiously, the leaves froze in the air.

A frantic voice broke the spell. "Jennet! I'm here, right next to you. Don't lose me again."

Jennifer!

I reached into the encroaching nothingness and felt a warm hand closed around mine. In the next instant, Jennifer materialized at my side.

"You did it!" she cried.

I stared at my surroundings in wonder, not yet fully grasping the new reality. The earth was at rest and blessedly quiet. The seasons had tumbled backward. The leaves were on the trees again, fresh and green, dozens of shades, and a riot of vibrant color bloomed on the roadside. Once again Huron Court had scrambled the seasons.

"Where are we?" I asked.

"On Huron Court," Jennifer said, "but I can't find the end of the road, or I should say the beginning?"

"I'm heading that way," I said. "I'm so happy to see you." I decided to pause all the questions except one. "Where's Molly?"

"She has a sore throat and feels nauseous. I told her to rest on the trail while I went for help. Then I saw you, but you slipped away. Somewhere." She broke off. "We have to get home before night. Our parents will be worried sick. Can you help us?"

Something felt off. "But you've been gone for many nights, Jennifer. For almost two weeks. You and Molly and Ginger. Your families are beyond worried."

Her eyes widened in disbelief. "No, that can't be. You're wrong. We just set out this morning. We just found Autumn."

I tried again. "Did you hear the wind? It stopped suddenly, but for a while it was horrible. Straight line winds. Like a tornado almost."

She shook her head. "There's just a light breeze. It feels good."

"That's true now, but didn't you notice it's summer again?"

She fell silent and looked at the green leaves as if seeing them for the first time, as if she were going to cry.

"Tell me what happened," I said, "then let's go back and get Molly and the dogs, and we'll go home."

Thirty-nine

Home.

How easy it was to say that word. How difficult to think of the home I'd left this morning with the leaves beginning to turn color and an autumnal crispness in the air. Was it now summer on Jonquil Lane instead of September?

We started walking back to where Jennifer had left Molly on Autumn's trail.

Jennifer had fallen silent, perhaps putting two and two together. She still looked puzzled.

"Tell me what happened," I repeated.

Finally she spoke. "We've been looking for Autumn, but you know that. This morning we packed a lunch and headed for Huron Court. It's the one road we hadn't searched."

I noticed her reference to the morning but didn't correct her. She wasn't ready to accept that she and Molly had been missing for days, courtesy of a road that had one more way of playing with time.

"Where Huron Court split in two, we decided to take the road on our left. There's nothing there, but we found a trail and decided to see where it led. It was hard seeing anything because of the fog."

I was wondering when the mist or fog would make its entrance.

"That's when Ginger found Autumn," she said. "The poor thing was starving, and her coat was a mess. We gave her our lunch, but then Molly started feeling sick. I was going for help but couldn't find the fork in the road. Then I saw you."

"The first time?"

"Yes. Just a quick glimpse, but it was clear. Then you vanished. So the next time I saw you, I grabbed your hand."

And pulled me into another season? Another time? Unfortunately, not the one I wanted.

Don't ask for too much, I told myself. At least she can see you, and you brought Misty with you.

"Where were the dogs all this time?" I asked.

"Sometimes they stayed with Molly. Sometimes they ran off in the woods to play, I guess."

"I'm asking because I saw Autumn near my house. When she didn't come to me, I followed her." I frowned, trying to call back the entire memory. "There was fog. I followed her..."

I broke off. Strands of the incident were dissipating. How had that pursuit ended? I couldn't remember the details. Pushing the effort aside, I said, "We have to get everybody together. Then we'll try to find the way home.

"Maybe I didn't walk far enough before," Jennifer said.

I didn't think that was the problem. But what was? Huron Court didn't want to release its captives?

I couldn't see the point of confusing the issue by telling Jennifer that the time was off. Way off. I could cross that bridge when I came to it.

She broke off and pointed to a stand of pines. "There's the trail. Jennet...You weren't serious about how long we've been gone, were you?"

"Dead serious," I said.

"I don't understand. I'll swear it's been just one day."

"Apparently one day on Huron Court is longer than twenty-four hours," I said.

~ * ~

We found Molly where Jennifer said she would be. With the way my life had been going, I was afraid she would be gone, but she sat on the ground, her back against the trunk of an old oak tree.

She didn't look well. Her face was pale and drawn, and her hair looked as if she had been constantly pushing it back from her forehead. Her face was flushed. Misty nudged her and stretched out at her side. Molly stroked the collie's head, then let her hand fall listlessly to the ground.

I knelt beside her, noting several red spots on her legs. She scratched at them. "Bug bites. Wish I'd worn jeans."

"Are you feeling better?" I asked.

"Not really. My throat hurts, and I'm warm, then cold. It came on so fast. I don't know what's wrong."

Neither did I, but Molly should see a doctor or at least be resting in her own bed.

"Are there any juice boxes left?" she asked. "I'm so thirsty."

"I think so." Jennifer reached into the repurposed shoe box that served as a lunch pail. "Here's one. Pineapple. We have bottled water if you're thirsty, Jennet," she added. "I wish we hadn't given Autumn all our sandwiches."

"I'm not hungry, but I'd like some of grandma's chicken soup," Molly said.

"Will you be able to walk..." I began.

"Don't leave me here!"

"We'll stay together," I promised. "One way or another. Molly, can you stand if we help you? And maybe walk?"

"I think so. I'll try."

"It'll be dark soon," Jennifer pointed out. "If we're going, we'd better get started."

I looked at the sky but saw no sign of a waning day. Perhaps night wasn't going to make an appearance in this timeline.

Ridiculous notion. But from the girls' perspective, the day had gone on without breaking, while back in the real world, the one I'd left, time marched on.

Maybe it wasn't such a ridiculous notion after all.

"What are we going to do, Jennet?" Jennifer asked.

I wish I had the answer. Whatever steps I took to try to extricate us from Time's death hold, we would still be in the wrong season. The wrong time.

But that meant the girls wouldn't have gone missing. Molly wouldn't be sick. I'd never met Linnea Wilmott, never searched for Autumn because she'd never been lost, and besides, I'd never heard of her. And I wouldn't have found myself on Huron Court in a treacherous windstorm.

Didn't it?

Keep thinking along those lines and you'll lose your mind.

Molly and Jennifer were counting on me to save the day. I needed inspiration quickly.

My heart skipped a beat at an ominous crashing in the woods. Ginger and Autumn leaped into the clearing, both dogs sporting burrs and leaves sticking to their coats and wagging their tails happily. Home from an adventure. Misty yelped a welcome but didn't leave Molly's side.

Our little company was complete, and I was the leader with no idea of what lay ahead.

Forty

A leaf fell from the oak tree, turned from green to gold in an instant, and swirled through the air before falling at my feet. Then another. And another. The cooling breeze gained strength and changed to wind.

It happened in the blink of an eye. Suddenly, the air was thick with falling leaves. They were all around us, and trees swayed ominously. Once again, we faced the danger of getting crushed.

"What's happening?" Molly cried.

Jennifer paused, the bottle of water halfway to her mouth, batting leaves from her face with her free hand.

"It isn't summer anymore," I said.

Molly was close to tears. "It's so cold. I'm freezing."

Was this new development good or bad? Impossible to tell, but if the season were changing again, time was changing with it. Soon I might be back in the time I'd just left. Back in the windstorm, this time with Molly and Jennifer and the dogs.

Which wasn't where I wanted to be, but Huron Court hadn't given me a choice. At least we were together, and it was clear we couldn't stay here.

The leaves kept falling, doing their crazy mid-air dance, gathering underfoot with alarming speed. The ones that brushed against my face had a sharp edge.

"We have to move. Now!" I looped Misty's leash around my wrist. "Jennifer, do you have Ginger's leash?"

She did. "Which way?" she asked.

The trail ran straight through the woods, from one end of the road to the other. "It doesn't matter."

She reached for the lunch box that held juice and water.

"No, leave it. Just hold on to Ginger."

Together we helped Molly stand and take a few steps. I hoped she would be strong enough to navigate the windstorm. I hoped Autumn would follow us. Hope, I realized, was all I had left.

The wind gave a low moan. I couldn't stop shivering, glad I had worn a dress with long sleeves this morning. How could the temperature drop so rapidly in so short a time?

"Where are we going?" Molly asked.

"To find the fork in the road."

And, if Fate were benevolent, to find our proper time.

~ * ~

We headed back to the road I was more familiar with, walking into the wind. Once we left the sheltering woods, the gusts were as strong as those I'd experienced before meeting Jennifer. But we managed. Both Jennifer and I held on to Molly, and we each led a dog. Our weight, combined with the weight of two adult collies ensured that we'd stay earthbound. Unless a tornado swept down on us.

Autumn raced ahead, often hidden by the wind-whipped leaf curtain that cut off our visibility.

If we didn't end up in our correct time, which was a possibility, I would have to explain what I didn't understand myself. Doubtless the girls still thought they'd only been away from home for a single day; and they didn't consider themselves missing. I knew exactly how long I'd been wandering in the wilds of Huron Court.

Didn't I?

Of course.

But why had I left home, taking only one of the dogs with me?

I felt as if I were trying to recall a dream, once vivid and compelling, now unable to withstand the morning light.

Something about fog and a house the color of the pink roses blooming on Camille's vine?

That was the pink Victorian, but it had burned to the ground long ago. In its place, hundreds of varieties of flowers grew wild and free.

Then something about a mirror? What?

Jennifer stumbled and promptly righted herself. Molly's grip on my hand tightened.

"A rock," Jennifer murmured. "I didn't see it."

Blown out from the woods, covered with leaves. Easy to miss unless you kept your eyes glued to the ground.

"How much further?" Molly asked.

"Not far," I promised. "We'll get there."

The road curved continually, and who knew what lay beyond each one? We had to keep going. Standing still wasn't an option. Nor was going back.

But wasn't the wind dying down? Just a little bit? Yes. A little. A teapot whistle instead of a howl and gradually nothing at all. Isolated splashes of blue, purple, and pink broke through the flying leaves.

Leaves? Only a few strays fluttered overhead. Then the air was empty, the ground unlittered. On our right, the tall flowers of the wildflower meadow moved languidly in a gentle autumn breeze. The pink house was gone.

"Look at the trees!" Jennifer cried.

They were green again. Well, not entirely. Ribbons of crimson and russet and yellow threaded through the green. The leaves of fall were nearing their peak. We were in the right season, and the air barely stirred. I could hear a bird singing.

Now if only the time was right. Our time.

"The storm's over," Molly said. "Good. I don't think I can walk another step. Can't we rest now? Just for a few minutes."

"Let's hurry home," Jennifer said. "We can rest later."

Forty-one

After what seemed like hours, we reached the fork in the road and, miraculously, didn't lose our season. Next stop, the lake, Sagramore Lake Road, and the girls' home.

We had lost Autumn again. I couldn't remember when I'd last seen her, but I consoled myself with the thought that she was resilient. She appeared to move between times. Which reminded me of my Autumn sighting this morning. Why couldn't I remember what came of it?

Think about that later.

As soon as the girls were safe in their homes, their parents could notify the police, after which whoever wanted to tackle the mystery of their long absence was welcome to it. All I would say was that I'd found them in the woods of Huron Court. On the trail. That was the truth, slightly edited.

The girls were devastated that Autumn had wandered off.

"Now we don't have a perfect record," Jennifer said. "No one will believe we found her."

"What if she lost her way back there in the windstorm?" Molly said.

Jennifer was quick to answer. "If you feel better, we can go look for her tomorrow."

What? No!

"I saw her running ahead of us," I said. "Don't give up. We may see her again."

And maybe she isn't meant to be found.

Their lament disappeared when we reached Sagramore Lake. A woman in jeans, her dark hair tied back with a scarf, was sweeping her front porch. She threw down her broom and rushed to intercept us.

"You're back!" she cried. "Jennifer! Molly! What happened to you?"

"It's a long story," I said. "For later."

Jennifer smiled, but Molly seemed to be on the verge of tears.

We kept walking. The woman, whom Jennifer addressed as Mrs. McAllister, stayed at our side, and before long a virtual parade accompanied us down the street. It seemed as if someone from every house came out to welcome the girls home—and to bombard them with questions. Molly's mother ran up to greet us and swept Molly into her arms. Both mother and daughter began to cry.

"Mom," Molly said. "I'm sick. My throat…"

"My baby!" Molly's mother cried. ""Who took you? Where were you all this time?"

"It wasn't that long," Molly said between sobs.

Then Jennifer's mother pulled in her driveway. Leaving the car door open, she rushed to Jennifer and embraced her. Suddenly, everyone was crying. With dogs barking and people talking over one another, Sagramore Lake Road had acquired the festive air of a block party.

It was a good time for me to take my leave of the happy reunion. Let the girls' families ask their questions and grapple with the answers. My own reunion waited for me in a green Victorian farmhouse on Jonquil Lane.

I gave Misty's leash a light tug. "We're going home," I said.

And, thank heavens, we're in our own time.

~ * ~

I couldn't have asked for a happier homecoming. The house sat quietly in a surround of autumn splendor. The stained glass between the gables had an enticing shine in the mid-afternoon sun, and the breeze had so light a touch I could scarcely feel it. The nightmare wailing and crashing was far in the past.

Best of all, my collies crowded at the front window, all of them barking, a sound that always lifted my spirits.

But why did their greeting seem especially poignant today? Because I feared I wouldn't make it through the windstorm that had ravaged Huron Court?

Really, Jennet, it was just wind.

Misty drank a half bowl of water and looked for her white goat while I looked at the clock. What had I planned to cook for dinner?

Nothing. I'd said goodbye to Crane and shortly after, spied Autumn and set out to coax her into the house and…

After that, everything was hazy. How had I gone from our property to a raging wind on Huron Court? Why had I taken Misty to Huron Court for that matter? I usually walked three dogs at a time.

Above all, why couldn't I remember?

I took a shower, applied fresh make-up, and changed into a blue shirtwaist dress. Still the details of the morning eluded me.

Think about dinner.

I found a casserole dish of stuffed cabbages in the refrigerator and baked two apple pies. Maybe if I kept busy, my memories would return.

Later, Camille came over with an enormous bouquet of black-eyed Susans. "I have so many and you just have the one plant. Or is it two? Anyway, something told me you'd like them. What have you been doing all day?"

The simple version?

"I took Misty for a walk and we found Jennifer and Molly."

I brought a vase from the cupboard and scissors to trim the flowers. For an instant an image sparked in my mind, then died.

"Thank God," Camille said. "Are they okay?"

"Jennifer is. Molly's complaining of a sore throat. It's a strange story. I'm not sure of the facts."

"Where were they?"

"Not far. On a trail off Huron Court. It's complicated," I added. "I should know more tomorrow."

"We'll read about it in the *Banner*. I guess it's true. All's well that ends well. You'll be getting the reward."

I hadn't thought of that. I didn't think any of the searchers did.

"I don't want it," I said. "I just want what I have."

Forty-two

What I wanted was Crane and my dogs under one roof and normalcy. And I wanted to be with them. Was that too much to ask?

By the time Crane came home, I had regained my equilibrium and energy, but not my memory of the early part of the day. I did recall a little, though. I'd heard a dog barking and seen Autumn briefly, but she hadn't come to me. Then I'd seen her on the trail with Ginger. For a while we'd all been together until the wind started to blow.

The unnatural wind. I also remembered struggling my way through a maelstrom of whirling leaves.

At one point we'd literally walked into another season, to our own time. By then Autumn was no longer with us. I'd left the girls in their parents' hands and gone home with Misty. There the memories stopped.

Crane shoved his way through the collie welcome committee and pulled me into his arms.

"I hear you found Jennifer and Molly, honey, but that's all anybody knows," he said. "I want the full story."

The details that I didn't have.

"Well," I said. "It's simple. I was out walking Misty and I ran into Jennifer."

"Where was this?"

"On Huron Court."

He fastened his frosty gray eyes on me. "You never take the dogs walking on Huron Court. You don't go there yourself."

"I did today."

I could tell he thought I was leaving out whole chunks of my narrative—and I was—but all he said was, "How did Jennifer and Molly get away from their kidnappers?"

"There were no kidnappers. They were looking for Autumn. They found her, too. Then Molly got sick and Jennifer got lost trying to get home."

"Lost on Huron Court?"

"That's what she said."

"But they were gone for days. Where were they?"

Tears burned in my eyes. Because Crane didn't believe me. Because I felt that he had turned into my interrogator. Because I didn't remember.

Why had I chosen Huron Court, of all roads in Foxglove Corners, for a walk with Misty?

"That's all I know," I said. "You'll have to get the rest of the details from the girls."

"Mac will. He's baffled. They went missing days ago, but they claim they were only gone since this morning."

"That's what they told me," I said.

"It doesn't make sense."

"But they believe it."

"Mac thinks they're covering up for someone. Or maybe someone's threatening them."

I was sure that Lieutenant Mac Dalby would have plenty of theories. Maybe he'd even come up with the right one.

"Let's just say it happened on Huron Court and leave it at that," I said.

~ * ~

Brent chose that evening to join us for dinner. He had heard of the girls' return. Practically everybody had, and the latest edition of the *Banner* wasn't even out yet.

Thank heavens for stuffed cabbages and the apple pies I'd baked.

"You say the girls were on Huron Court, but I've been back there several times and never saw them," he said.

"Are you looking for trouble, Fowler?" Crane demanded. "Didn't we agree to stay away from that whole infernal area?"

"I don't think so," I said, but they ignored me.

"I'm curious about that mist," Brent said. "I want to see it again. Besides, I own property on Huron Court. I like to check on my wildflower meadow every now and then."

That reminded me. Brent hadn't been able to remember where he'd been or what he'd done when he'd gone missing.

"Do you want to lose your memory again?" I asked.

"That probably won't happen, but if it does, I'll deal with it."

"I can't remember everything about this morning," I admitted. "It's like the day began when I ran into Jennifer, and that can't be right."

"You have too much on your plate," Brent said. "That time traveling gal, school, the lost dog...By the way, how did you let her get away?"

"Autumn wasn't on a leash," I said. "She was used to running free, and it was so terribly windy."

"Today?" Crane said. "Not where I was."

"It's always windy in Foxglove Corners."

Crane looked at me. After a moment, he said, "You don't forget things, Jennet."

I only wished that were true.

Brent said, "Do you think the girls were lost in time?"

"They must have been, but they're convinced they were only gone for a day. Molly says she wants to feel better for the first day of school. She's missed it by two weeks."

"She can't argue with the calendar or the rest of the world," Crane pointed out.

"No, or that school's been in session without her."

As soon as their lives settled down, which I hoped would be soon, I was going to talk to them, to point out what must have happened.

"The mysteries just keep coming," Brent said.

I nodded. "One after another. My whole morning is a mystery."

Crane covered my hand with his own. "It'll come to you, honey. I agree with Fowler. You've been trying to do too much. Slow down a little. Concentrate on what's important."

That was good advice, if not particularly practical. My plate would only get fuller as the novelty of a new school year wore off and the troublemakers unsheathed their claws. So what if I hadn't found Linnea, and Autumn had slipped away from me? I had brought the girls home. That was a major accomplishment.

Forty-three

I read the story in the *Banner* at Clovers on Tuesday. It was skimpy with no mention of the number of days the girls had been missing, nor of the reason for their disappearance. The investigation was ongoing.

'Ignore what you don't know and hint at a follow-up' appeared to be the reporter's approach.

Annica set a lime cooler in front of me, and I set the paper aside. When I'd told her about the girls' bizarre belief that they'd only been gone for a day, she immediately said, "They got all tangled up in time. No wonder no one could find them."

"Something similar may have happened to me, too."

"You disappeared? When?"

"No, but I can't remember part of yesterday morning. I don't know why I took Misty walking on Huron Court."

"That doesn't sound like something you'd do."

"I was there, though. That's a fact."

"If you weren't, Jennifer and Molly would still be lost."

"That's true."

"So think of it as an angel's plan. We'll have to rename Huron Court. How does Weird Road sound?"

"Too tame. I'm just glad to be out of that windstorm and back to normal. Sort of."

"Then you can help me with my latest problem," she said. "That redheaded witch, Alethea, has decided to be my friend. She wants to give me a bridal shower."

"What? I'm your maid of honor."

"I told her you planned to give me one, but she says Brent has lots of friends you don't know, and they all want to welcome me to the crowd." She rolled her eyes. "As if that's my great desire."

"Don't believe her," I said. "Alethea always has an agenda."

"I told her I didn't need two showers. She says you can be a cohostess with her."

"That'll never happen."

"What should I do if she insists?"

I hated to see Annica floundering. That wasn't like her. She should be able to deflect Alethea's manipulations.

"You already declined," I reminded her.

"She'll never let it go."

"It's too nice a day to ruin with Alethea's foolishness." I stirred the whipped topping into my drink. I kept thinking that each lime cooler was the last of the season, but it was another gorgeous fall day, and I had reason to celebrate.

"We'll think of something to stop her in her tracks," I said.

It was bound to be easier than dealing with the secrets of Huron Court.

~ * ~

Whenever supernatural events threatened to overwhelm me, I sought the company of Lucy Hazen. In spite of my resolve, I couldn't leave the mystery of my lost hours behind me. I knew that I was mentally sound. At least I hoped so. Maybe the answer lay in the teacup. If not, I'd have a pleasant visit with Lucy and Sky.

Crimson, orange, and bright gold splashed the trees that grew along Spruce Road. When I'd come this way for Lucy's tea party, back before school began, there'd been only a narrow ribbon of yellow woven through the green. Now I was traveling in a virtual grove of gold. Goldengrove unleaving. Leaves blew across the road, a few of them sticking to the windshield.

That day seemed so long ago. So much had happened to me since I'd met Linnea Wilmott and, I assumed, also to her.

I had an absurd fancy that Linnea was following me on Spruce Road and down the long conifer-lined driveway to Dark Gables. She could be anywhere.

Autumn color and golden sunshine bathed Lucy's house in brightness. Lucy and Sky were on the porch, Lucy reading and Sky chewing a bone.

"How lovely to see you, Jennet," Lucy said. "I expect you're busy now that school started."

Sky dropped her bone, and I gave her a quick pat on the head.

"They let us out early to make up for the night we'll have to come back for a parents' meeting."

"I've been curious about Molly and Jennifer. There's not much in the papers."

"Hardly anything." I told her what I knew.

"Huron Court," she murmured. "Say no more."

"My problem is I have no memory of why I went there," I said.

"Let's go inside and you can tell me about it over tea."

Once seated on the wicker sofa in the sunroom waiting for the water to boil, I told my story for the second time that day. How strange it must sound.

"Maybe I'm getting forgetful," I said. "It scares me."

'Haunts me' would be a better way to describe the feeling. I could understand Brent's wondering what he did when he was missing, although he seemed to have put it behind him.

"It's curious," Lucy said, "but I no longer sense danger stalking you. Perhaps you'll remember in time."

"I hope so," I said. "As of now, those hours are a blank."

"There must be a reason for the blackout."

"What could it be?"

"One day it'll all be clear."

I was vaguely aware of the teakettle's whistle. It seemed far away—in another room. Good grief, was my hearing going too?

Lucy set a plate of sugar cookies on the table and poured the tea. "Let's see what your future holds."

With my luck, all the leaves would fall out and I'd have no future. That had happened to one of Lucy's friends once, and it had left Lucy so shaken she had temporarily abandoned her readings.

I peered over Lucy's shoulder at what to me was a mishmash of leaves. I could never see the patterns that spoke to Lucy.

"This is a good cup," she said after a moment's perusal. "I see your wish, but here's something unusual. I see a curve."

"A curve? What does that mean?"

She pointed to a lone leaf next to the three little dots that signified my wish. "Possibly you'll veer from your ordained path."

That didn't sound too terrible. In school, I was always changing direction in midstream.

"Your immediate future looks tranquil," she added. "I'd say you deserve a time of peace."

She only mentioned Linnea once. "I'm afraid we'll never hear from her again."

"Didn't you say she calls when she wants something?"

"She can hardly call from the past, if that's where she is. It's best if you put her out of your mind. It's out of your hands. It was never in your hands to begin with."

Linnea wasn't easy to forget, though. I couldn't file her under 'Unsolved Mysteries' and move on, not while her collie remained among the lost.

Autumn, I thought, where did you go?

~ * ~

That evening, I looked for my time travel books. I'd last seen them neatly stacked on the coffee table. They weren't there now, but my Kindle was, along with yesterday's *Banner*, my American Lit textbook, and Misty's white goat toy.

"Did you see those books I picked up at Green's?" I asked Crane.

"Not lately. Did you look in the bookcase?"

We had several bookcases in various rooms throughout the house, but I remembered leaving them on the coffee table so they'd be handy if I wanted to reread them.

Uh, maybe I did.

As it was late, almost time to start dinner, I didn't make a proper search. They had to be somewhere in the house. Misplacing three old-time books wasn't a calamity.

I'd look for them tomorrow.

Forty-four

Before I had a chance to visit Molly and Jennifer, they came to see me, bringing Ginger as always. We sat on the porch drinking lemonade. Their signature enthusiasm had deserted them. Molly still looked wan. They were clearly troubled, and I wasn't surprised.

"We don't understand what happened to us," Jennifer said. "They say we were gone for two weeks. We weren't. They all think we're lying. Even Mom."

"So, we pretend we don't remember," Molly added.

"It's Huron Court," I said. "Some say it's evil."

"How can a road be evil?" Jennifer asked. "It's just a road."

"I won't go that far, but strange things happen there. I suppose you've heard of time travel stories."

"Sure," Molly said. "Like *Back to the Future*. That's my favorite movie. And *Somewhere in Time*. Someday, we're going up to Mackinac Island when they all dress up in period costumes."

Good. That was a basis on which to build.

"People have been known to fall into another time when they're on Huron Court," I said. "It happened to me."

Molly said, "For real?" But Jennifer only stared at me.

"I think that's what happened to you."

"But we were only there one day. We never left Huron Court."

"You don't remember leaving it," I said. "Maybe you didn't, but several days went by. Time plays by different rules on that road."

"If we traveled in time, why didn't we go someplace cool?" Molly asked. "Like to the future. Maybe we could have traveled to another planet."

"Because...I don't know how to answer that except to say that you weren't in control of where you went or how long you stayed. The road was."

Jennifer frowned. "Now I really don't understand."

I remembered Lucy's advice and passed it on. "Try to put it out of your mind. Stay away from Huron Court and you should be okay."

"We have to find Autumn," Molly said.

"Still?"

"If that road is evil, we can't leave her there."

"No, I guess you can't, but go in a group."

"We can do that," Jennifer said. "We'll go with the Dogfinders."

~ * ~

That evening I looked all over for Linnea Wilmott's books. Where could I have put them? Was it possible...? A troubling idea lodged in my mind and refused to leave.

Did they still exist?

Well, of course they did. I had purchased three books, read them, and set them aside. Now they were nowhere to be found.

It was like the time I couldn't find Linnea's contact information and wondered if the whole incident had been eliminated from life's canvas.

Playing with time could have unforeseen results.

"I don't know where they could be," I said to Crane.

"They're in the last place you'll think to look."

"Maybe, and maybe we have a black hole in the house."

I fell back on the idea that capricious Time had erased them, going round and round with it until I grew dizzy. If Linnea hadn't traveled to a certain year, 1920, for example, she wouldn't have written them.

But then, how would I have found them growing old and deteriorating in the Green House of Antiques?

Let's say that someone else, a non-time traveler named June Summers, was the author. Then they would be on the coffee table. Wouldn't they?

I was an English teacher with a good knowledge of time travel literature, not a scientist. If I kept trying to find answers for the unanswerable, I'd work myself into a headache. It was better to push the problem to the back of my mind with the lost hours.

As Crane assured me, someday I'd find them.

~ * ~

The next day, I had just gone into the kitchen when my cell phone rang. Brent's voice boomed out loud and clear. He was in a state of high excitement.

"You have to see what I discovered, Jennet. You'll never believe it."

I closed my book and gave him my full attention.

"I drove out to the wildflower field to take a few pictures and saw the mist begin to form on the trail," he said.

I held my breath. Bent had gone to Huron Court again? Crane would be furious.

"You didn't go too close, I hope."

"I did. I have some great pictures on my phone."

"I guess nothing bad happened or you wouldn't be calling."

"I've been sitting here watching it for two hours, Jennet. The sun is shining, but the mist hasn't burned off. It looks solid. I'll bet I couldn't put my fist through it."

"Don't even try."

"Come see it," he said.

I looked around my kitchen. I'd just brewed a pot of tea and cut a slice of coffee cake. Sky lay under the table, and Misty was sitting by my side waiting for the inevitable crumb to fall. I could almost see Crane. He'd be home soon. I was safe and happy.

"No," I said.

"The mist isn't going anywhere. This is your chance to solve the mystery."

"Which part of it, exactly?"

"All of it."

I envisioned an apple, round, juicy, and caramel-covered. Eve couldn't resist the apple. Neither could Snow White. How could I?

Easily.

"If you've been looking at the mist for two hours, it's time to come home," I said. "While you still can."

He said, "It's so beautiful, Jennet. It's like all the trees are iced over, and it stops right at the edge of the woods. Wait! Something's moving. I can't... my God!"

The connection died.

"Brent?"

Hastily, I tapped his number and listened to the beginning of his hearty greeting.

He was in trouble. The man who was always there for others had a major problem, even if he had invited it into his life with open arms. Even if it meant venturing into forbidden territory, I had to help him.

But I wouldn't go alone.

"Misty," I said.

She sprang up and dashed to the hook where I kept the dogs' leashes. It was as if she had understood the gist of Brent's message.

Of course she had. My beautiful psychic collie.

I could only do this with her.

Forty-five

I didn't see Brent's car, but the mist lay heavily over Autumn's trail. I wouldn't describe it as a block of ice, though. It looked like regular mist, white and breaking into narrow gauze-like strips that wrapped themselves around the trees.

An unnatural mist that existed alongside a bright harvest sun. Brent was right. It stopped at the woods' edge. Yes, unnatural, but that wasn't news.

Where was Brent?

His vintage white Plymouth with its long green fins would be difficult to miss. Unless it was beyond one of the road's many curves. In which case I'd have to drive to the end of Huron Court—to the cemetery.

I gazed at the rows of autumn-hued wildflowers, some of them so tall a man could hide behind them, but Brent wasn't there; nor was his car parked at the trail. I had pictured him stationed at the trail's exit watching the never-dissolving mist. For two hours? Had it bewitched him?

I replayed our conversation. How sure was I that Brent was in trouble? He'd said, 'my God' before our connection failed. That didn't necessarily mean 'Help!' Could the mist have begun to dissipate after which he'd taken my advice and gone home?

Not after telling me that I had to see his discovery.

But he couldn't call me.

I didn't know what to think, but I had a feeling he hadn't left Huron Court. I couldn't stay there and wouldn't venture onto Autumn's trail, even though the mist was quite thin now. Even though apparently Brent had.

Especially now that the wind was picking up.

And a leaf fell.

And the day was rapidly losing its brightness.

"Let's get out of here," I said and stepped on the ignition.

Nothing happened. The engine was as dead as Brent's cell phone. Was the whole of Huron Court an electronics-unfriendly zone? This had never happened before. At least I didn't think so.

An image of myself trying to start the car on another day formed in my mind and dissolved.

Maybe it had. How could I be sure of anything these days with my memory so unreliable? What did I do then? Probably asked Crane to look at it. I couldn't remember.

All around me leaves began to fall. I was trapped. I had trapped myself.

You fool!

I was the one bewitched. Bedeviled, I should say. I knew the dangers of traveling on Huron Court. I'd said over and over that I wouldn't go anywhere near that accursed roadway.

But if my friend needed my help...If there was even a chance that he was in danger...

What's done was done. I'd made it through one windstorm. I could take on another. Grabbing Misty's leash, I opened the door, brushed a rush of leaves from my face, and started walking.

~ * ~

The force came out of nowhere, careened into my space, and barreled into my right side, sending me flying through the air. I landed at the side of the road in a mound of fallen leaves where I lay stunned as the pain caught up to me.

Out of nowhere. My space. My side. Dear God.

What had hit me? It felt like a steel house. Or a car. I was walking on a road, so it must have been a car.

But where had it come from? I hadn't heard the hum of an engine or the blare of a horn and hadn't sensed an impending menace. How could a car materialize in thin air?

Misty! The force had torn the leash from my hand. I had to find her.

I tried to move my arms and turn, tried to rise but vertigo overcame me. I closed my eyes and felt my awareness drift away.

The leaf-covered ground made a soft bed. I longed to lie still and let the leaves fall on me, bury me, save me from the pain that squeezed my ribs with every breath.

Eventually I was able to stand and take a few steps back to the road. Then I was walking again, moving through the pain and the leaves, calling Misty.

The wind pushed me on. If I could find the end of the road. Or the beginning. My sense of direction was skewered. Was I going north or south? Toward the lake or the cemetery? I had to escape from Huron Court.

Leaves thronged through the air, blinding me. Walk in a straight line, I told myself. *Don't veer off into the woods or you'll be lost.*

Veer?

Lucy had seen a curve-shaped leaf in my teacup. 'Perhaps you'll veer off in a different direction,' she'd said.

Her powers had failed. She'd promised me a time of serenity. Instead, my future offered pain and chaos and leaves—leaves falling endlessly, battering me, coming alive, each leaf a sharp-toothed entity cutting my skin like a razor.

In the heart of the chaos, I heard a dog barking.

~ * ~

The wind and the leaf storm were gone, and a weak light filtered through the brush that grew alongside the road. A dark-haired woman with wide streaks of gray in her hair and a worried expression on her face leaned over me.

"What have I done? I'm so, so sorry."

I tried to move my hand but something lay on top of it. Something soft that whimpered.

Misty?

"You ran into me with your car," I said.

"Yes, but I didn't have a choice. I'm so sorry."

"Couldn't you see me?"

"Not until it was too late."

The car had grazed me. A car driven by a distracted driver who assumed she was alone on a country road. It could have been so much worse. Anger boiled up in me. I didn't think any bones were broken. I was only badly bruised. Only?

I couldn't hold back the tears. Still whining, Misty licked my face.

I remembered the nightmare impact and the crackling of leaves as I was hurled into them.

I needed to be in tip-top shape to teach my classes.

"Can you sit up?" the woman asked. "Here, I'll help you."

"My dog. Is she hurt?"

"I'm sure she's okay, but she's worried about you."

I reached out and found Misty's head, stroked it, and felt marginally better. "I'm all right, girl, I said. "It's all right."

But was it? My words were for Misty. Inside I was seething.

The woman helped me to stand, but after a moment, I had to sit again.

"I'll drive you to the hospital," she said. "If that's your car back on the road, you can have it towed."

Until that moment I'd forgotten Brent.

"I came to meet my friend here but couldn't find him," I said. "Did you see a white Plymouth with green fins?"

"Fins?"

"It's a vintage car."

"Not lately," she said.

"Or a handsome man with dark red hair?"

"No one. Just you and me."

I looked at her more closely. Gray-streaked black hair, features vaguely familiar, light lines around the eyes and mouth as if she'd drawn them with an eyebrow pencil, dark red lipstick.

She looked like an elder relative of someone I'd known briefly.

"Have we met before?" I asked.

"We have, recently," she said. "Did you forget? I'm Linnea Wilmott."

Forty-six

"I made it back," Linnea said. "At long last."

Linnea. It made sense, in a weird kind of way. But she looked older, by at least twenty years. I'd last seen her only a few months ago. Who knew that time travel would be aging?

She helped me into a yellow Plymouth and opened the back door for Misty. She wanted to take me to an emergency room. I wanted to go home. We agreed that we needed to leave Huron Court far behind before some unwelcome change in season or time prevented it.

"I couldn't avoid the collision because that was the moment I came through, and there you were with your dog," she said.

"In the wrong place at the wrong time."

Again I thought how close I'd come to dying under the wheels of Linnea's time-traveling vehicle.

I remembered Lucy telling me that Linnea's goal was to make a different life decision and added, "Were you able to change your future?"

"It was a good idea, but it didn't work out," she said. "Fate doesn't like to be thwarted. Since I realized that, I've been practically living on this road, driving up and down, praying I'd return to my own time, but

I never did. It was always the wrong year. Until today. I even tried to get your attention a couple of times," she added.

With the object left under the angel statue and the time travel book in Miss Eidt's attic. Desperate, uninspired ways almost certainly doomed to fail.

"How was I supposed to help you?" I asked.

"I don't know. Maybe you couldn't, but I just wanted someone to know what had happened to me, where I was."

I stared ahead through a moderate fall of leaves. This was natural for the season, and the trees weren't bowing down in the wind. So far, so good.

We passed the fork in the road and before long approached the exit or entrance, depending on your perspective. I could almost smell the lake water and taste the freedom.

"You haven't mentioned your collie, Autumn," I said.

"I was wrong about that, too. She didn't cross over with me."

"Autumn is here, in our time. We've seen her, but she won't let herself be rescued. She's waiting for you."

For the first time, Linnea smiled. "I was resigned to losing my girl. From now on, finding Autumn is my top priority."

~ * ~

I had dozens of questions, but Linnea seemed disinclined to indulge in further conversation. That was all right, because she claimed to have no knowledge of the most important matter of all: Brent.

A grim suspicion nagged at me. What if he had driven into the past while Linnea had crossed over to the present? That meant he was lost again. Well, he'd been determined to pursue the mystery of the mist. It was said that curiosity killed the cat. It certainly hadn't been kind to Brent.

I couldn't imagine where else—or when else—he'd be, but as soon as I had access to my cell phone, I'd try to contact him at the barn or at his home.

As we passed Sagramore Lake, Linnea said, "Are you sure you don't want to go to Emergency, Jennet?"

"I just want to go home," I said, envisioning a shower, a cup of tea, and pain pills. Misty was on her feet in the back of the Plymouth gazing out the window. She would be dreaming of home, too. Fresh water, bones and treats, and her beloved white goat toy.

"So do I," Linnea said. "When I woke up this morning, it was 1960. I think I'm suffering from a kind of jet lag.

~ * ~

Home. Blessed home. Collies in the window. Everything where I'd left it. My cell phone on the counter where I had foolishly left it. Collies crowding around me. Bliss.

I frowned. Why was I surprised? I'd only left the house a few hours ago. What would have changed?

The closest I came to Brent was listening to the greeting on his cell phone. I left him a message but doubted his phone would work in 1960 or 1940 or wherever he'd landed.

After a shower, the pain pills, a change of clothing, and a muffin snack that I didn't share with the dogs, I felt worse. Probably I should go to the hospital after all. I'd ask Crane to take me.

Crane...He wouldn't be happy with me or with Brent, who had gotten himself lost again. Well, I'd deal with that bridge when I came to it.

Later that afternoon, I made another search for Linnea's time travel books but didn't find them. Darn. I'd forgotten to ask her if she'd stayed in one time long enough to write them.

Would the mysteries never end?

Not as long as Huron Court existed. I amused myself with the dark fantasy of setting fire to the road. Perhaps a nice conflagration would rid the entire area of its strangeness.

Not that I'd do that, of course. But I wouldn't be sad if lightning struck a tree and did the job for me.

As the afternoon wore on, I kept thinking about Brent and periodically tried to contact him.

He's gone, I thought. Linnea's found, but Brent's lost.

Annica would be devastated. As for myself, I couldn't imagine Foxglove Corners without Brent Fowler.

Forty-seven

I knew Crane wouldn't be pleased by my latest misadventure. He wasn't. I could tell by the frost forming in his eyes and his stern deputy sheriff's tone.

"You're not the world's savior, Jennet," he said. "Why didn't you call me?"

Why hadn't I? I couldn't remember now. It would have made more sense than striking out on my own.

"I will the next time," I promised.

"There won't be a next time. Limit yourself rescuing to collies. That's safe."

Ha! I didn't say that out loud.

"It was just a terrible coincidence that I ran into Linnea Wilmott or she ran into me," I said. "It won't happen again. Not in a trillion years."

"Maybe not, but don't test it. I assume Ms. Wilmott has lost her enthusiasm for time travel."

"It appears so. Now if you can find Brent, we'll all be happy."

"First things first," he said. "I'm taking you to Emergency. It's non-negotiable."

"I won't argue. Maybe they have stronger pain medication."

"After you get a clean bill of health, we'll have dinner out."

An evening with my husband in a restaurant made a trip to the hospital more palatable. As long as they didn't admit me.

~ * ~

They didn't. I was badly bruised (which I knew) but otherwise unharmed. The doctor told me to take Tylenol.

Afterward, we dined on steak with creme caramel for dessert, and my sleep that night was fitful. My dreams overflowed with leaves—falling, burning, scenting the air with…Marshmallow?

I woke up craving a fancy sundae, and as soon as I took care of the dogs and said goodbye to Crane, I headed for Clovers.

Annica was doing her best to pretend that all was well. Once again, Brent had failed to meet her after her shift, and no one knew where he was. She wore black, though, and looked like a mourner.

"He's gone again," she said.

"Crane will find him." I told her what I knew, which included Linnea's catastrophic return. Catastrophic for me, that is.

"I didn't realize I was marrying a daredevil," Annica said. "What if he doesn't come back?"

"Linnea did."

"I hope he didn't go where she did."

She glanced at Marcy who nodded, then sank into the booth opposite me. "I don't want to lose him. I love him."

Marcy glided up to us, order pad and pen in hand. "Can I get lime coolers for you girls?"

"It's so chilly today," I said. "How about hot chocolate? Okay, Annica?"

At Clovers they served it with mini-marshmallows.

She nodded.

"Let's trust Crane to bring Brent home and talk about something happy, like your shower. Alethea's not on the guest list."

"I hope there'll be a wedding," Annica said.

~ * ~

On Sunday, Lucy hosted another get together for Linnea and me. I was looking forward to it. Maybe I could ask my questions, after which

I'd part company with Linnea. I hoped that after today I would never see her again. In fairness, I should blame Huron Court for my various aches and pains, but human nature being what it is, I blamed Linnea.

She apologized again for the collision. Deciding to be gracious, I said, "It wasn't your fault."

Lucy said, "Linnea, will you tell us what happened with your—er—young man?"

Linnea sighed. "It didn't go as planned. I arrived a year too late. He had already met another girl and given her an engagement ring. My decision didn't matter. Timing is everything," she added.

Surreptitiously I studied her face. She was still pretty, but she had definitely aged in a few short months. I wondered if she was aware of it. She must be.

"I still think we could have had a happy life together," she said.

"Maybe," Lucy said, "but it's always best to leave the past where it is and look to the future. There are plenty of fish in the sea."

"That's good advice."

I wondered if she'd take it. To change the subject, I said, "I read your books, Linnea."

"My children's books?"

"No, the time travels. Didn't you write them when you were in the past?"

She shook her head. "I was too busy trying to find the way home to write. I did some reading. though."

She wasn't June Summers, then. I was wrong. Well, it wasn't the first time. Which didn't alter the fact that the books I'd bought at the Green House of Antiques were still missing.

Linnea said, "I've been thinking. What I went through would make a good story. Now that it's over and I'm safely home. I know what my next project will be."

"That's right," Lucy said. "Every single experience is grist for the author's mill. Let me tell you how I got the idea for my current book..."

Instead of listening, I was wondering what new place I could look for my lost time travels.

~ * ~

Crane was right. The books were in the last place I'd think to look, in the basement, behind boxes of Christmas decorations. I almost didn't recognize them as they had been shredded. More accurately chewed.

Which dog was responsible for the damage and smart enough to hide the evidence? It could only be Candy, but the mischief had occurred days ago. She'd have long since forgotten her naughtiness.

With a sigh, I swept the mess into a trash can and calculated the worth of the books she'd destroyed. They were vintage volumes, possibly one of a kind. Even if they hadn't been written by Linnea Wilmott, they held some value.

The only remaining mystery was what had attracted her to these particular books when there were hundreds of others in the house. That was one I could never solve.

Oh, well, dogs will be dogs, and Candy will be Candy. I could never stay mad at her.

Forty-eight

Brent came home on a dreary October day of wind and falling leaves. He returned with no fanfare and no preliminary phone call, but he brought a shopping bag of treats for the collies and a spectacular bouquet of lilies, roses, carnations, and black-eyed Susans. As a peace offering, I surmised.

Crane hung his green suede jacket in the closet. "You'd better have a good excuse for dragging Jennet into danger again, Fowler." There wasn't the slightest hint of humor in his tone.

"Annica told me what happened to you, Jennet," Brent said. "I'm sorry, but I can explain everything. I know you'll understand." He handed me the bouquet.

"Go ahead. Explain."

He stashed the bag on the coffee table and tried to give all the dogs an equal amount of attention.

"We were talking on the phone when, lo and behold, I caught sight of Autumn tramping in the woods."

"Wasn't there a thick mist on the trail? Like a block of ice?"

"She just walked out of it. I called her, and she took off like a rocket. I got in my car, and it started snowing. You can guess the rest.

Unfortunately, I could.

"This time I remember everything," he said. "My wildflower meadow was gone. Violet's house was there, but it was empty. It looked abandoned. I spent two nights in one of the bedrooms. When I woke up this morning, the snow had melted. I got in my car and drove straight home."

"Annica must be overjoyed."

"She is, but here's something weird. I took dozens of pictures of the mist, but when I checked my phone, all I saw were woods."

"Well, it's Huron Court," I said.

He shrugged. "Tell me. How did I lead you into danger?"

"You told me that I had to see something. Then the connection died. Naturally, I thought something had happened to you."

"It was just an expression," he said. "How could I know you'd drive out to meet me? Can't we let bygones be bygones?"

"This time."

"Nice save," Crane said. "Don't let it happen again."

"That's good, because I don't see that I did anything wrong. And damn it—I was so close to having Autumn. Close doesn't count."

"Now that Linnea is home, she'll turn up. It's just a matter of when."

"Great," he said. "What do you have for dinner?"

While Crane and Brent talked in the living room, I trimmed the stems in my bouquet, breathing in the sweet fragrance of orange roses, yellow lilies, spicy white carnations, and black-eyed Susans. No perfume could compete with their scents.

The black-eyed Susans were larger than the ones that grew in Camille's garden, and perfect with glossy leaves that had never been nibbled by a bug.

Were they fragrant?

Rolling white mist and a sable and white collie. Camille and her marvelous garden of many colors, my frantic search for a mirror in the pink Victorian and the joy of seeing Misty's reflection and my own.

Every lost memory spilled out into my awareness like treasures from a magic pitcher. How impulsively I'd rushed out into the embrace of another season, another time, another challenge.

As Lucy had predicted, my memories had returned in their own time. I would have been completely happy except for the unsettling knowledge that the mist had followed me to Jonquil Lane, to my own backyard, and somehow left me and Misty invisible. Wasn't it supposed to stay on Huron Court? Was I ever going to be safe again?

Well, I would figure it out another day. Lucy would help me. In the meantime, I had a story to tell. And what a story!

But Misty and I had been rendered invisible? No one had heard our voices? We had walked through a crowd of sunbathers on the beach and no one was aware of us? Who would believe a story so outrageous?

Crane would. Brent would. Leaving the flowers on the cupboard, I hurried into the living room, interrupting Brent's fox hunting anecdote.

"Do you guys want to hear a fantastic story?" I asked.

~ * ~

Although Linnea had been searching for Autumn, in the end it was Molly and Jennifer who found her. She was padding along on the beach while they were walking with Ginger. This time she didn't run away.

She knew Linnea had returned and trusted the girls to take her home. After all, she knew them. She had stayed with them for a while on the trail.

Linnea set out for Foxglove Corners as soon as Jennifer called her with the good news.

It was a day of joy and gold. Everything in my view had turned from bright to radiant. The sun, Camille's six potted chrysanthemums on the porch of the yellow Victorian, the leaves on the linden trees, Autumn's fur, and the light haze that lay over Jonquil Lane.

While we waited for Linnea, Molly brushed Autumn's thick coat until it sparkled.

"She's such a pretty girl," Jennifer said, "but she's too thin."

She was, dangerously so, and perpetually hungry. "She'll soon be eating good food, and she'll be happy," I pointed out.

We would never know if Autumn had made a den on the trail or if she moved back and forth in time, as I suspected. It didn't matter, because now she was mere minutes away from her home.

When Autumn spied Linnea's Plymouth, she dashed out to meet it and almost knocked Linnea back into the car as she tried to stand.

Linnea hugged her, hiding her face in Autumn's white ruff. All she said was, "My precious little girl."

It was enough.

Against all odds, a woman and her dog had been reunited. I had come through an incredible adventure to resume my happy life. God was good, nature was calm, Time was benevolent, and the story had ended well.

Meet Dorothy Bodoin

Dorothy Bodoin lives in Royal Oak, Michigan, with her blue merle collie, Layla. On graduating from high school, she obtained a stenographer's position at Chrysler Corporation where she worked for six years, two of which were spent in southern Italy. After earning bachelor's and master's degrees in English literature at Oakland University, she began a second career as a high school English teacher. After retiring, she began a third career as a novelist, specializing in her favorite genre—mystery—and writing about her life-long love, collies.

Other Works from the Pen of Dorothy Bodoin

Treasure at Trail's End (Gothic romance) - The House at Trail's End seemed to beckon to Mara Marsden, promising the happy future she longed for. But could she discover its secret without forfeiting her life?

Ghost across the Water (romantic suspense) - Water falling from an invisible force and a ghostly man who appears across Spearmint Lake draw Joanna Larne into a haunting twenty-year-old mystery.

Darkness at Foxglove Corners - Foxglove Corners offers tornado survivor Jennet Greenway country peace and romance, but the secret of the yellow Victorian house across the lane holds a threat to her new life. (#1)

Winter's Tale - On her first winter in Foxglove Corners Jennet Greenway battles dognappers, investigates the murder of the town's beloved veterinarian, and tries to outwit a dangerous enemy. (#3)

A Shortcut through the Shadows - Jennet Greenway's search for the missing owner of her rescue collie, Winter, sets her on a collision course with an unknown killer. (#4)

Cry for the Fox - In Foxglove Corners, the fox runs from the hunters, the animal activists target the Hunt Club, a killer stalks human prey on the fox trail. (#2)

The Witches of Foxglove Corners - With a haunting in the library, a demented prankster who invades her home, and a murder in Foxglove Corners, Halloween turns deadly for Jennet Greenway. (#5)

The Snow Dogs of Lost Lake - A ghostly white collie and a lost locket lead Jennet Greenway to a body in the woods and a dangerous new mystery. (#6)

The Collie Connection - As Jennet Greenway's wedding to Crane Ferguson approaches, her happiness is shattered when a Good Samaritan deed leaves her without her beloved black collie, Halley, and ultimately in grave danger. (#7)

A Time of Storms - When a stranger threatens her collie and she hears a cry for help in a vacant house, Jennet Ferguson suspects that her first summer as a wife may be tumultuous. (#8)

The Dog from the Sky - Jennet's life takes a dangerous turn when she rescues an abused collie. Soon afterward, a girl vanishes without a trace. Ironically she had also rescued an abused collie. Is there a connection between the two incidents? (#9)

Spirit of the Season - Mystery mixes with holiday cheer as a phantom ice skater returns to the lake where she died, and a collie is accused of plotting her owner's fatal accident. (#10)

Another Part of the Forest - Danger rides the air when a kidnapper whisks his victims away in a hot air balloon, and a false friend puts a curses on a collie breeder's first litter. (#11)

Where Have All the Dogs Gone? - An animal activist frees the shelter dogs in and around Foxglove Corners to save them from being destroyed. Running wild in the countryside, they face an equally distressing fate and post a risk to those who come in contact with them. (#12)

The Secret Room of Eidt House - A rabid dog that should have died months ago from the dread disease runs free in the woods of Foxglove Corners, and the library's long-kept secret unleashes a series of other strange events. (#13)

Follow a Shadow - A shadowy intruder haunts Jennet's woods by night, and a woman who can't accept the death of her collie asks Jennet to help her find Rainbow Bridge where she believes her dog waits for her. (#14)

The Snow Queen's Collie - A white collie puppy appears on the porch of the Ferguson farmhouse during a Christmas Eve snowstorm. In another part of Foxglove Corners a collie breeder's show prospect disappears. Meanwhile, the painting Jennet's sister gave her for Christmas begins to exhibit strange qualities. (#15)

The Door in the Fog - A wounded dog disappears in the fog. A blue door on the side of a barn vanishes. Strange wildflowers and a sound of weeping haunt a meadow. The woods keep their secret, and a curse refuses to die. (#16)

Dreams and Bones - At Brent Fowler's newly purchased Spirit Lamp Inn, a renovation turns up human bones buried in the inn's backyard, rekindling interest in the case of a young woman who disappeared from the inn several decades ago. As Jennet tries to solve this mystery, she doesn't realize it may be her last. (#17)

A Ghost of Gunfire - Months after gunfire erupted in her classroom at Marston High School, leaving one student dead and one seriously wounded, Jennet begins to hear a sound of gunshots inaudible to anyone else. Meanwhile, she resolves to find the demented person who is tying dogs to trees and leaving them to die. (#18)

The Silver Sleigh - Rosalyn Everett was missing and presumed dead. Her collies had been rescued, and her house was abandoned. But a blue merle collie haunts her woods and a figure in bridal white traverses the property. (#19)

The Stone Collie - Jennet's discovery of a collie puppy chained in the yard of a vacant house sets her on a search for a man whose activities may threaten Foxglove Corners' security. Meanwhile, horror story novelist Lucy Hazen is mystified when scenes from her work-in-progress are duplicated in real life. (#20)

The Mists of Huron Court - The house was beautiful, a vintage pink Victorian in a picturesque but lonely country setting, and the girl playing ball with her dog in the yard was friendly, suggesting that she and Jennet walk their dogs together some time. Jennet thinks she has made a new friend until she returns to the house and finds a tumbling down ruin where the Victorian once stood and no sign that the girl and dog have ever been there. ((#21)

Down a Dark Path - What hold does the pink Victorian on Huron Court have on Brent Fowler who is determined to re-create the home of long-dead Violet Randall? When he disappears, could he have been cast adrift in time? (#22))

Shadow of the Ghost Dog - An invisible dog grieves inside the house chosen as a setting for the movie based on Lucy Hazen's book *Devilwish*, and a landscaper unearths a human skeleton in the backyard while planting shrubs. (#23))

The Dark Beyond the Bridge - The discovery of a secret ghost town in a densely rural area of Michigan's lower peninsula leads to mystery and danger for Jennet Ferguson and her friends. (#24)

The Deadly Fields of Autumn - An antique television set that airs an obscure Western at random times and a woman who disappears with her newly-adopted rescue dog draw Jennet into a puzzling mystery. (#25)

The Lost Collies of Silverhedge - Collie breeder Madselin Rivard was dead, leaving her prized, valuable collies uncared for in their kennel. Jennet and her friends rescue five of them, but eight remain unaccounted for. (#26)

All the Pretty Little Collies - Danger stalks the collies of Foxglove Corners when an unknown villain begins tossing poisoned meat into their yards, and a girl with a winning blue merle collie is warned via threatening messages to withdraw her dog from competition or risk the consequences. (#27)

Phantom in the Pond - Brent Fowler's plan to open a house for geriatric collies goes awry when strange things begin to happen in his newly-purchased country estate. (#28)

Challenge a Scarecrow - Scarecrows that guard a dangerous secret and a woman who believes she has brought her dog back to life add up to a frightening and deadly month for Jennet Ferguson. (#29)

The Dog Who Ran with the Sleigh - The apparition of an old-fashioned horse-drawn sleigh on a snowy road sends Jennet Ferguson over a deep slope into danger and possible death. (#30)

In the Greenwood He Was Slain - A search for four collie puppies abandoned on a country lane leads Jennet to a mysterious house in the woods, and a story of love, betrayal, and murder. (#31)

So Long at the Park - The search for a collie stolen from her ex-pen during a collie event challenges Jennet to solve a baffling mystery and ultimately to stay alive. (#32)

Letter to Our Readers

Enjoy this book?

You can make a difference.

As an independent publisher, Wings ePress, Inc. does not have the financial clout of the large New York publishers. We can't afford large magazine spreads or subway posters to tell people about our quality books.

But we do have something much more effective and powerful than ads. We have a large base of loyal readers.

Honest reviews help bring the attention of new readers to our books.

If you enjoyed this book, we would appreciate it if you would spend a few minutes posting a review on the site where you purchased this book or on the Wings ePress, Inc. webpages at:

https://wingsepress.com/

Thank You

Visit Our Website

For The Full Inventory
Of Quality Books:

Wings ePress.Inc
https://wingsepress.com/

Quality trade paperbacks and downloads
in multiple formats,
in genres ranging from light romantic comedy
to general fiction and horror.
Wings has something for every reader's taste.
Visit the website, then bookmark it.
We add new titles each month!

Wings ePress Inc.
3000 N. Rock Road
Newton, KS 67114

Made in the USA
Monee, IL
30 November 2023